APR  S0-AJY-160

NO LONGER PROPERTY OF
THE SEATTLE PUBLIC LIBRARY

APR 2 7 2023

CRAB & SNAIL
THE EVIL EEL

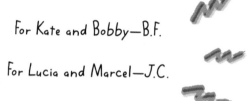

For Kate and Bobby—B.F.

For Lucia and Marcel—J.C.

HarperAlley is an imprint of HarperCollins Publishers.

Crab and Snail: The Evil Eel
Text copyright © 2023 by Beth Ferry
Art copyright © 2023 by Jared Chapman

All rights reserved. Printed in Italy. No part of this book may be used or reproduced in any manner whatsoever without written permission except in the case of brief quotations embodied in critical articles and reviews. For information address HarperCollins Children's Books, a division of HarperCollins Publishers, 195 Broadway, New York, NY 10007.

www.harpercollinschildrens.com

ISBN 978-0-06-296219-5 (p-o-b)
ISBN 978-0-06-296220-1 (pbk.)

Typography by Chelsea C. Donaldson
23 24 25 26   RTLO   10 9 8 7 6 5 4 3 2 1
❖
First Edition

CRAB & SNAIL

THE EVIL EEL

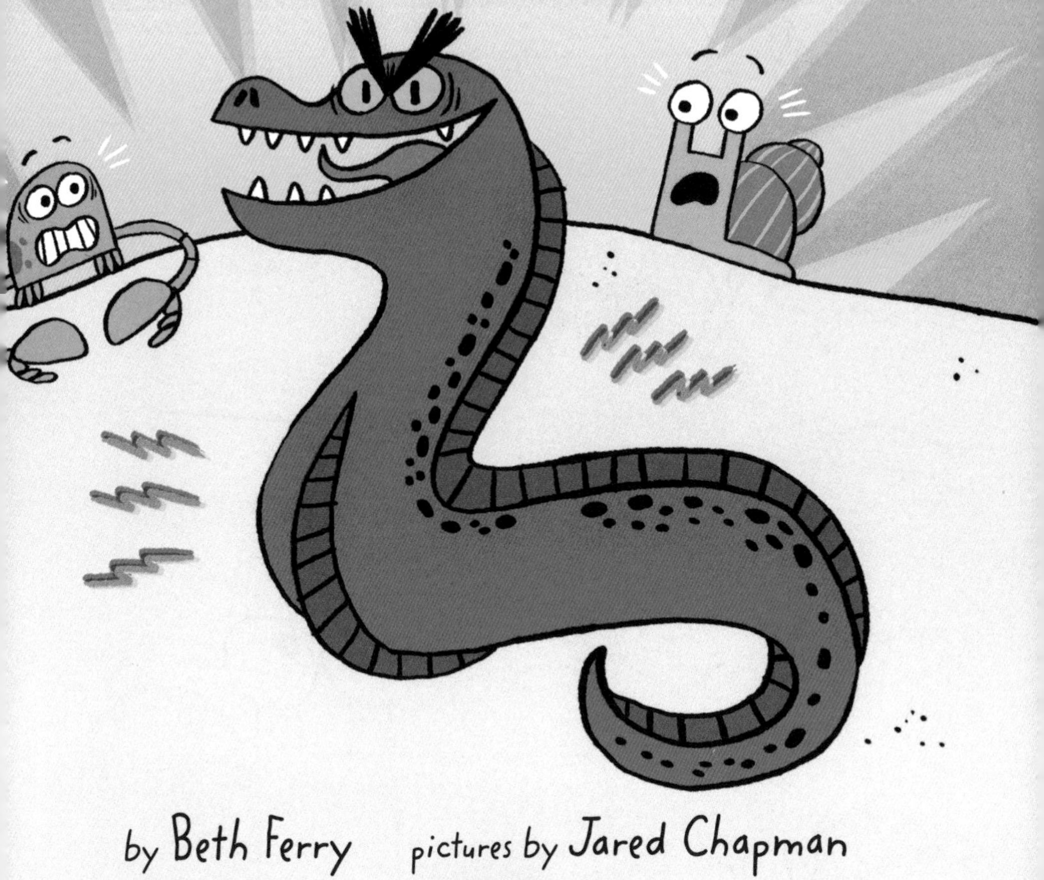

by Beth Ferry pictures by Jared Chapman

HARPER alley
An Imprint of HarperCollinsPublishers

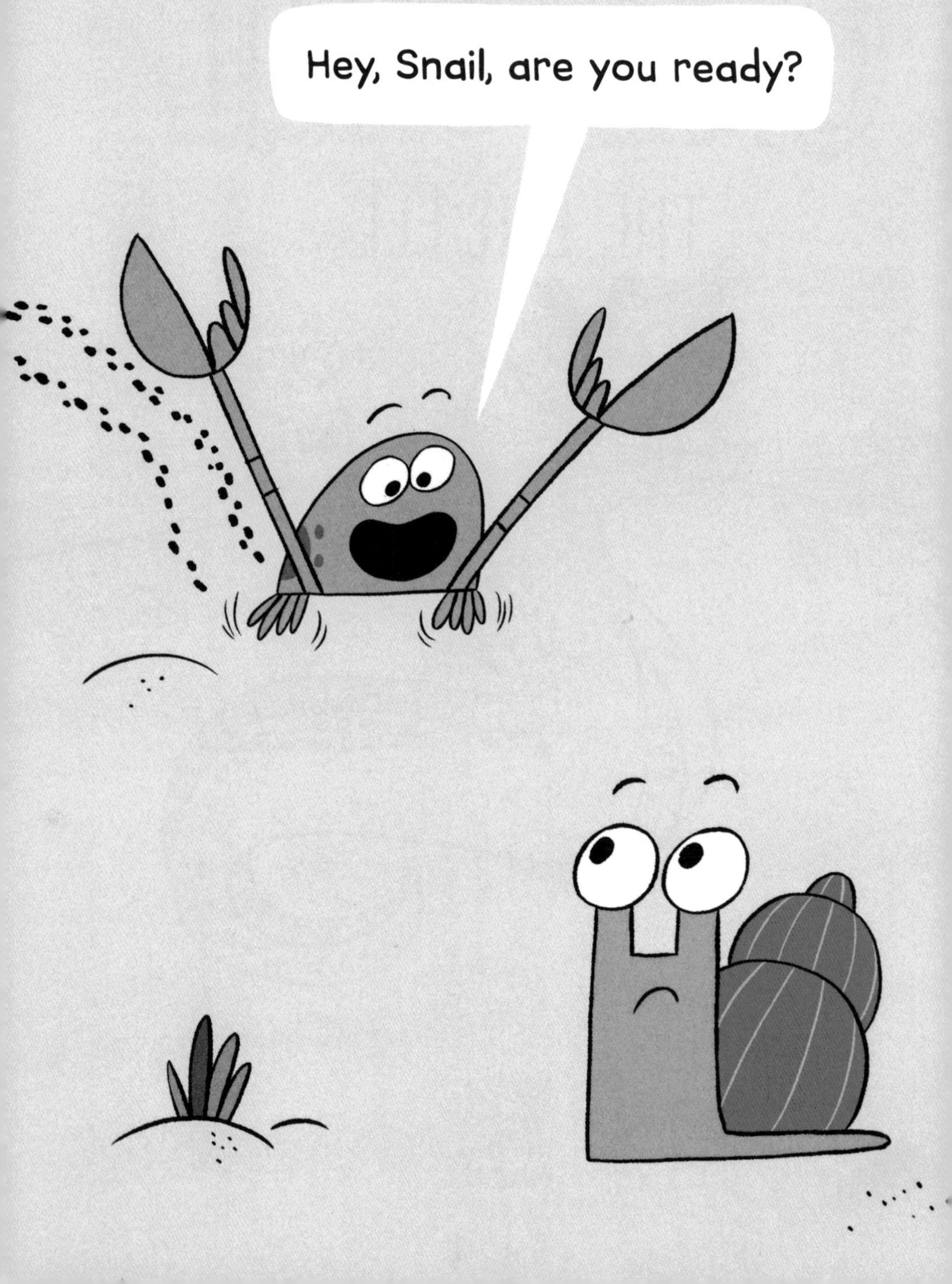
Hey, Snail, are you ready?

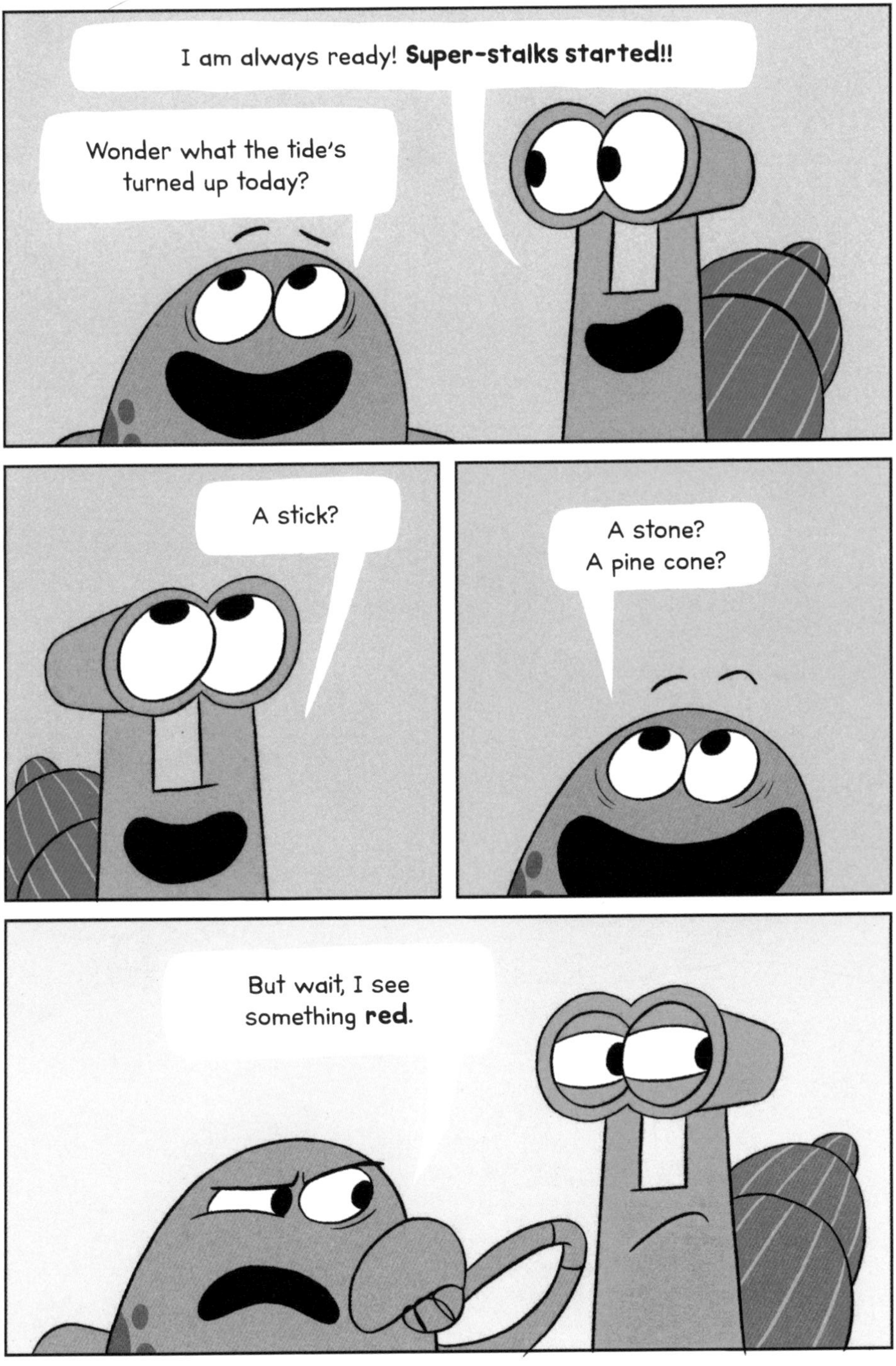
Wonder what the tide's turned up today?
I am always ready! **Super-stalks started!!**
A stick?
A stone? A pine cone?
But wait, I see something **red**.

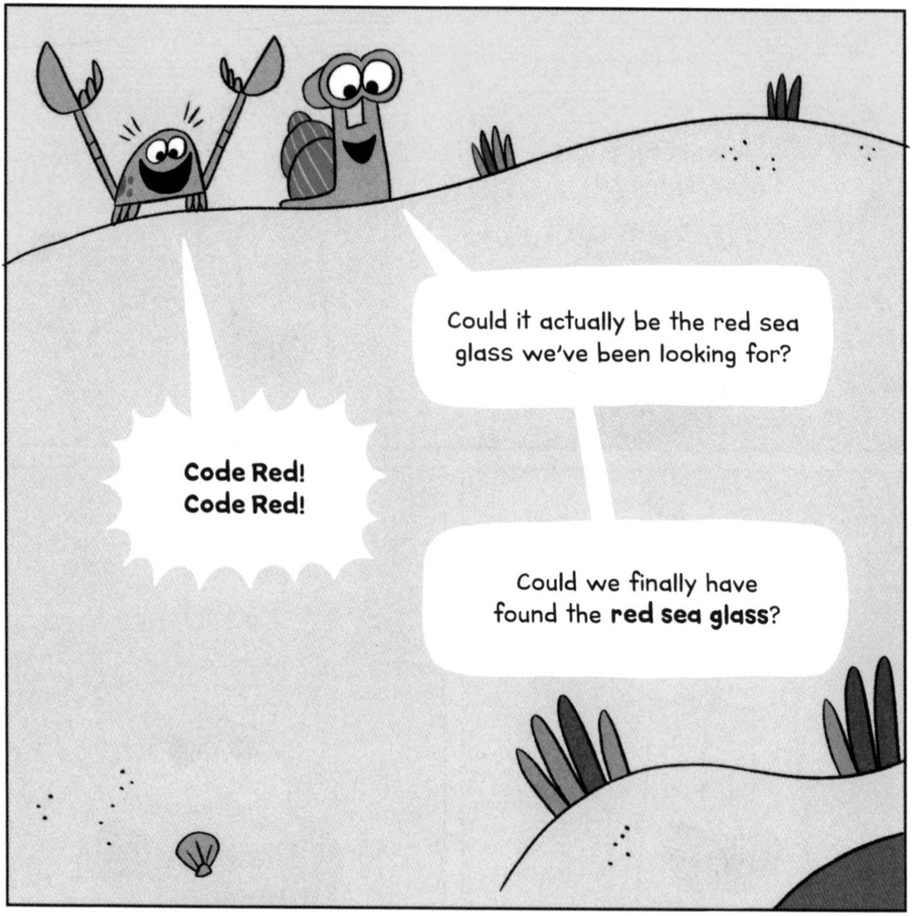
Code Red!
Code Red!
Could it actually be the red sea glass we've been looking for?
Could we finally have found the **red sea glass**?

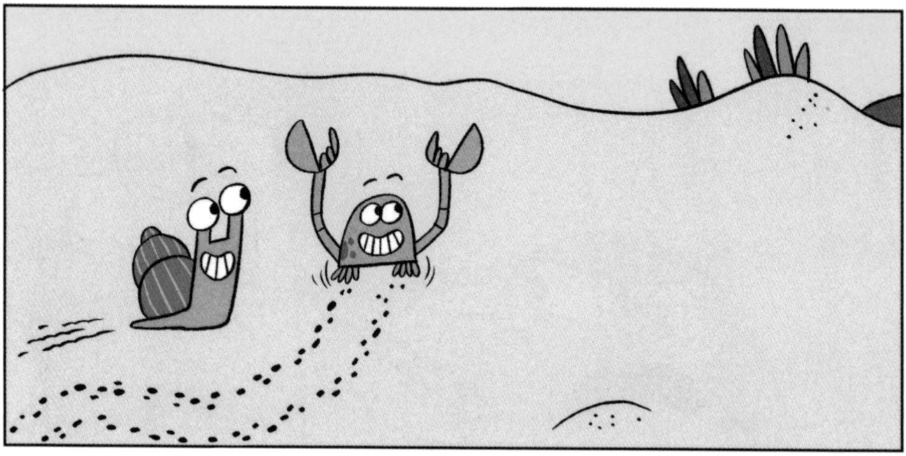

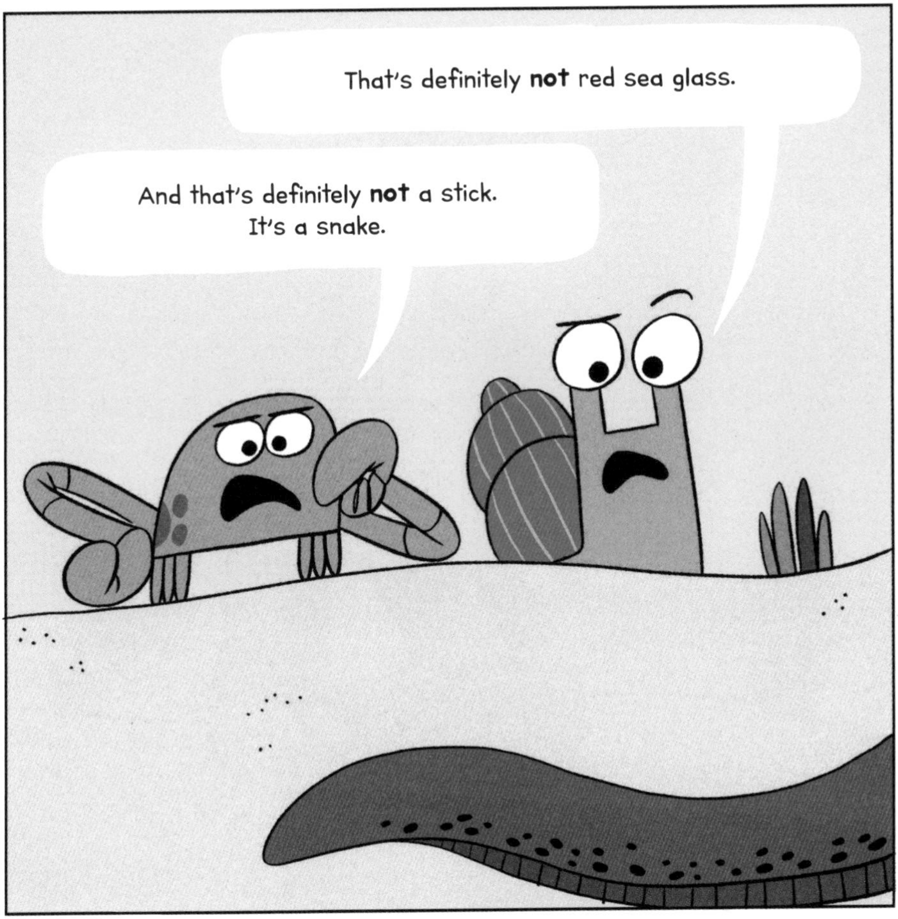
That's definitely **not** red sea glass.
And that's definitely **not** a stick. It's a snake.

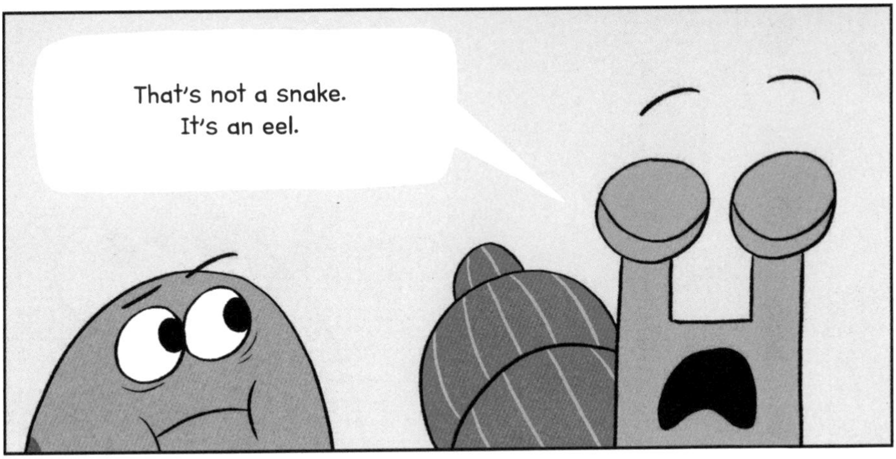
That's not a snake. It's an eel.

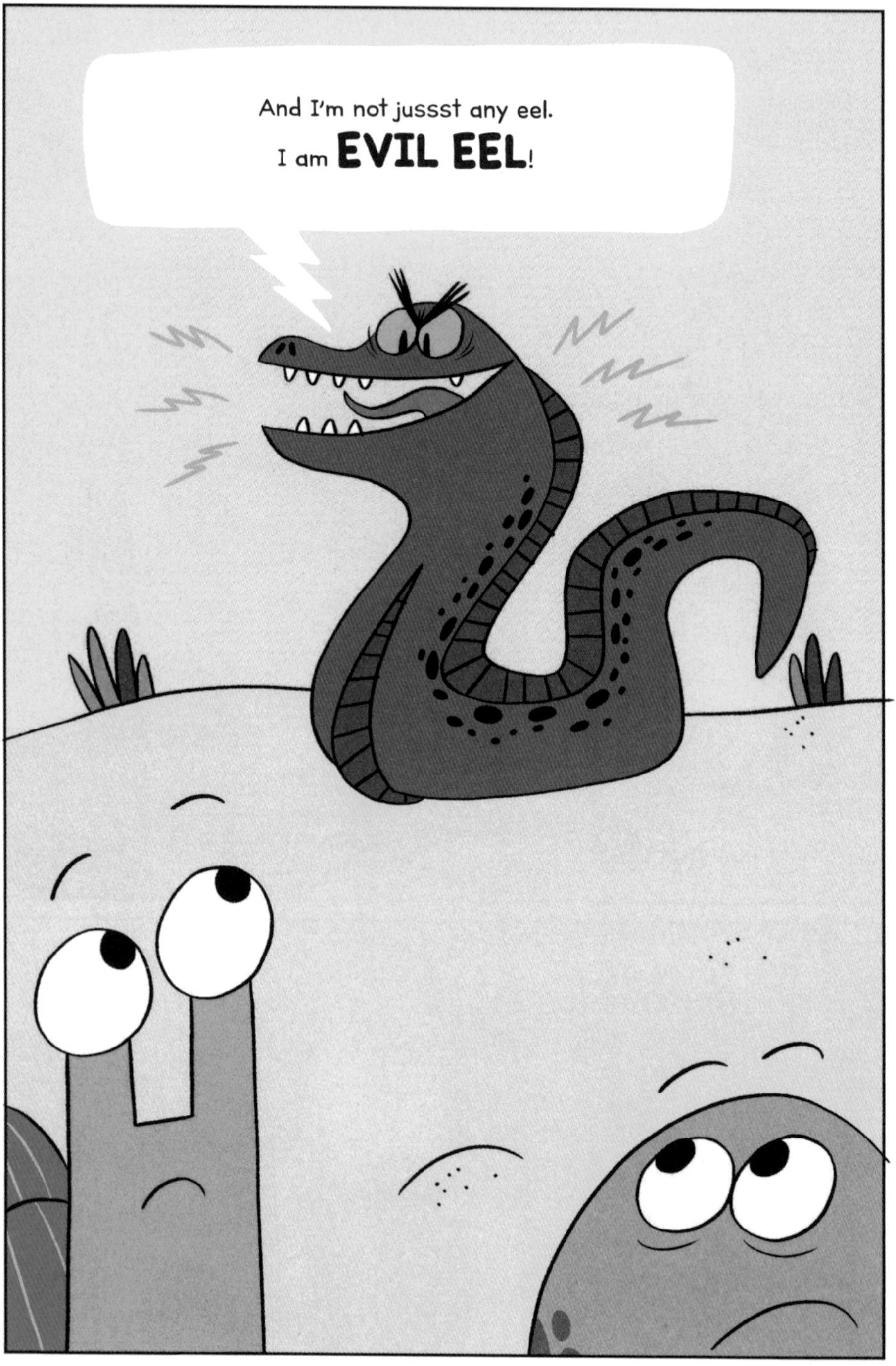
And I'm not jussst any eel.
I am EVIL EEL!

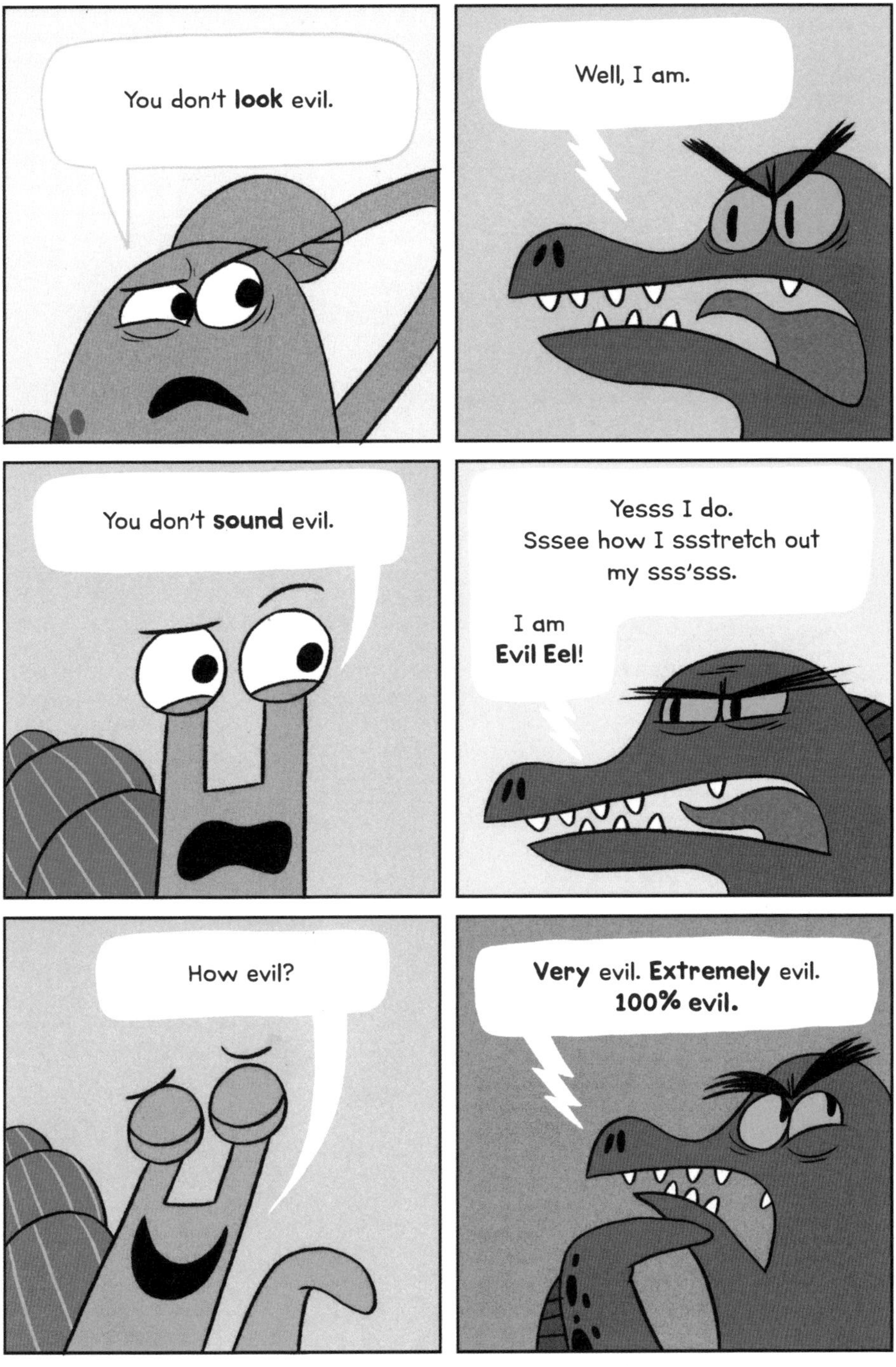
You don't **look** evil.
Well, I am.
You don't **sound** evil.
Yesss I do. Sssee how I ssstretch out my sss'sss.
I am **Evil Eel**!
How evil?
Very evil. **Extremely** evil. **100% evil.**

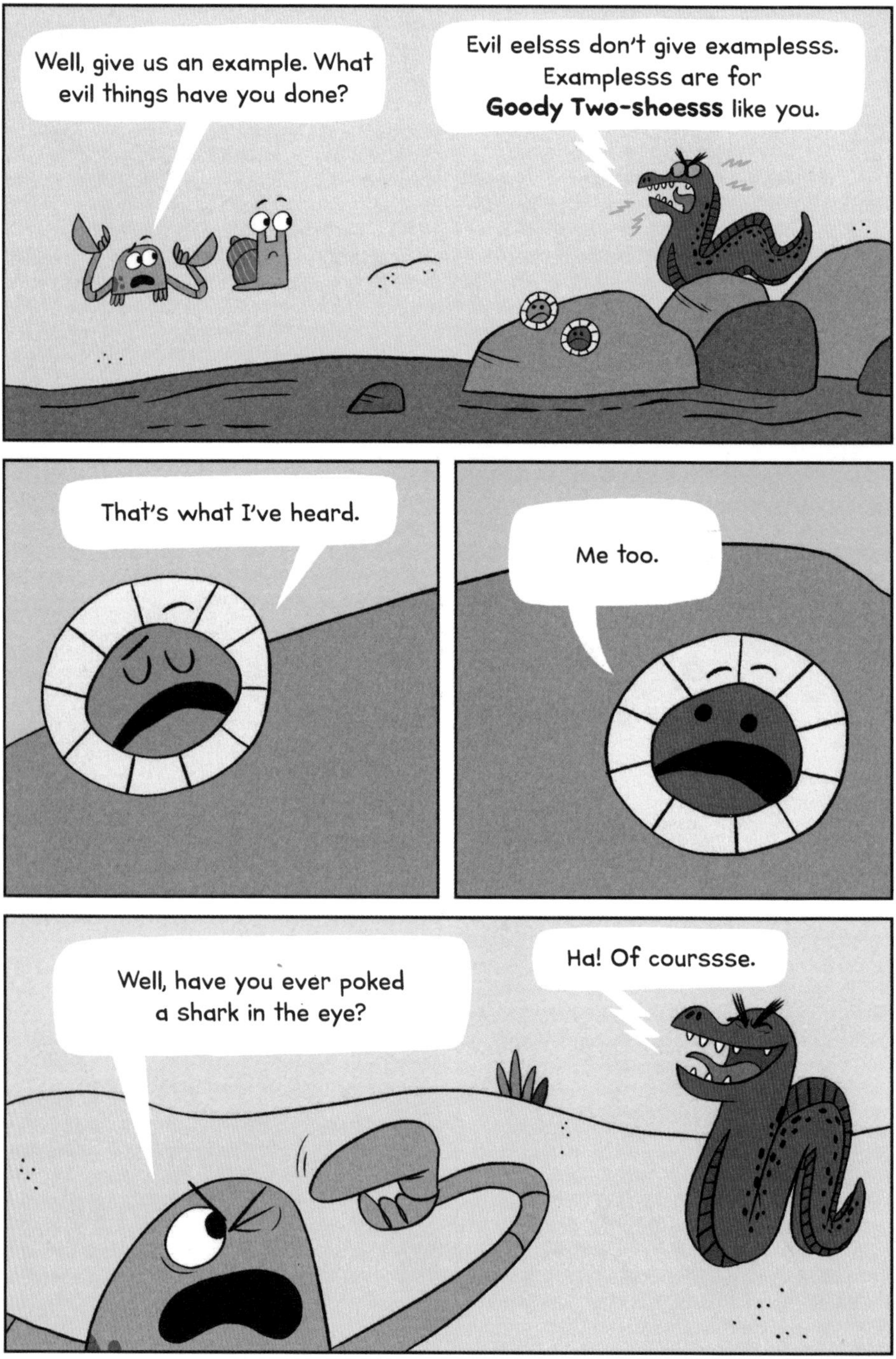
Well, give us an example. What evil things have you done?
Evil eelsss don't give examplesss. Examplesss are for **Goody Two-shoesss** like you.
That's what I've heard.
Me too.
Well, have you ever poked a shark in the eye?
Ha! Of coursssse.

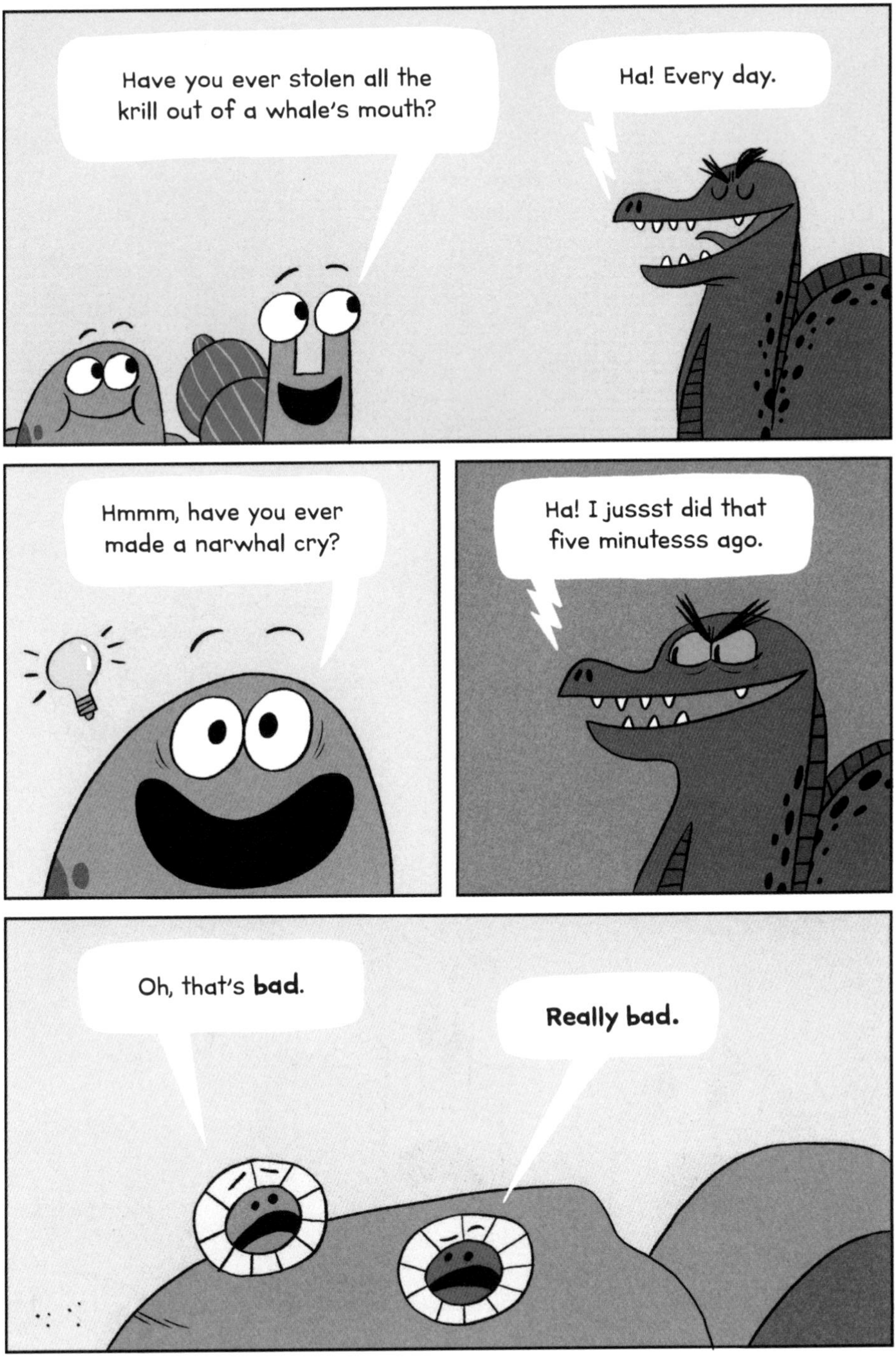
Have you ever stolen all the krill out of a whale's mouth?
Ha! Every day.
Hmmm, have you ever made a narwhal cry?
Ha! I jussst did that five minutesss ago.
Oh, that's **bad**.
Really bad.

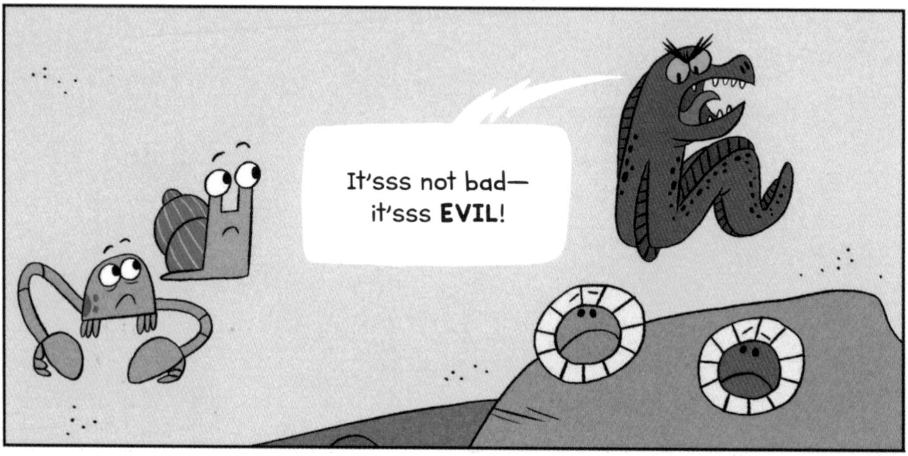
It'sss not bad—
it'sss **EVIL**!

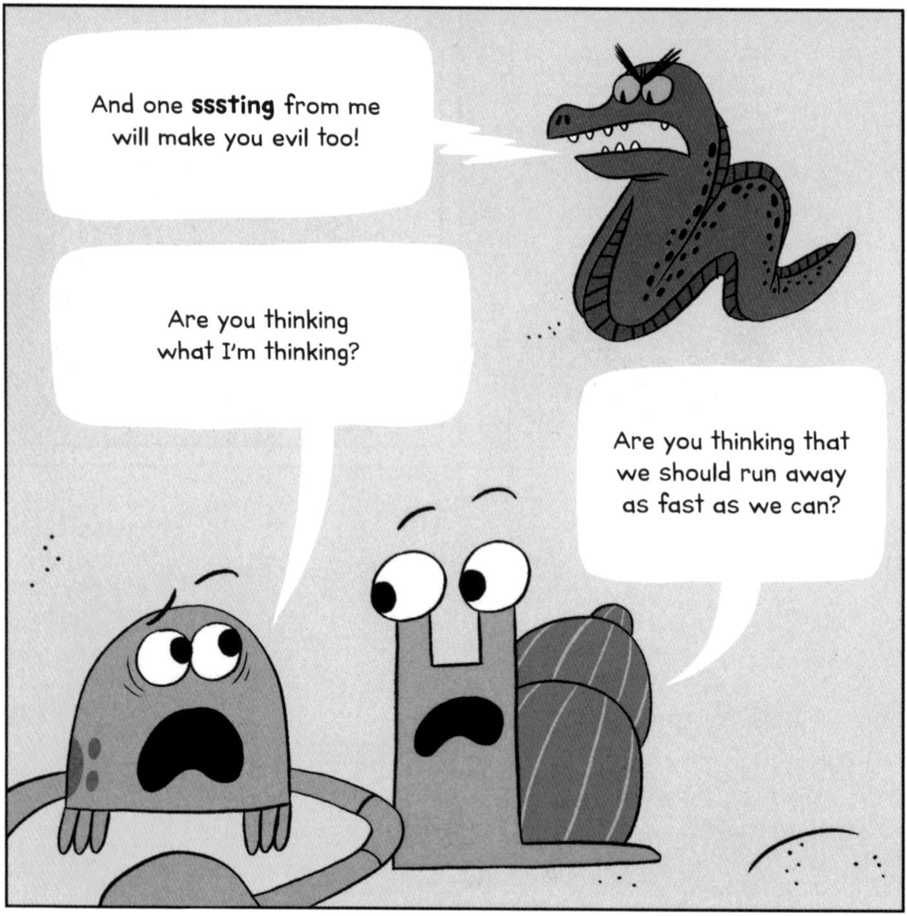
And one **sssting** from me
will make you evil too!
Are you thinking
what I'm thinking?
Are you thinking that
we should run away
as fast as we can?

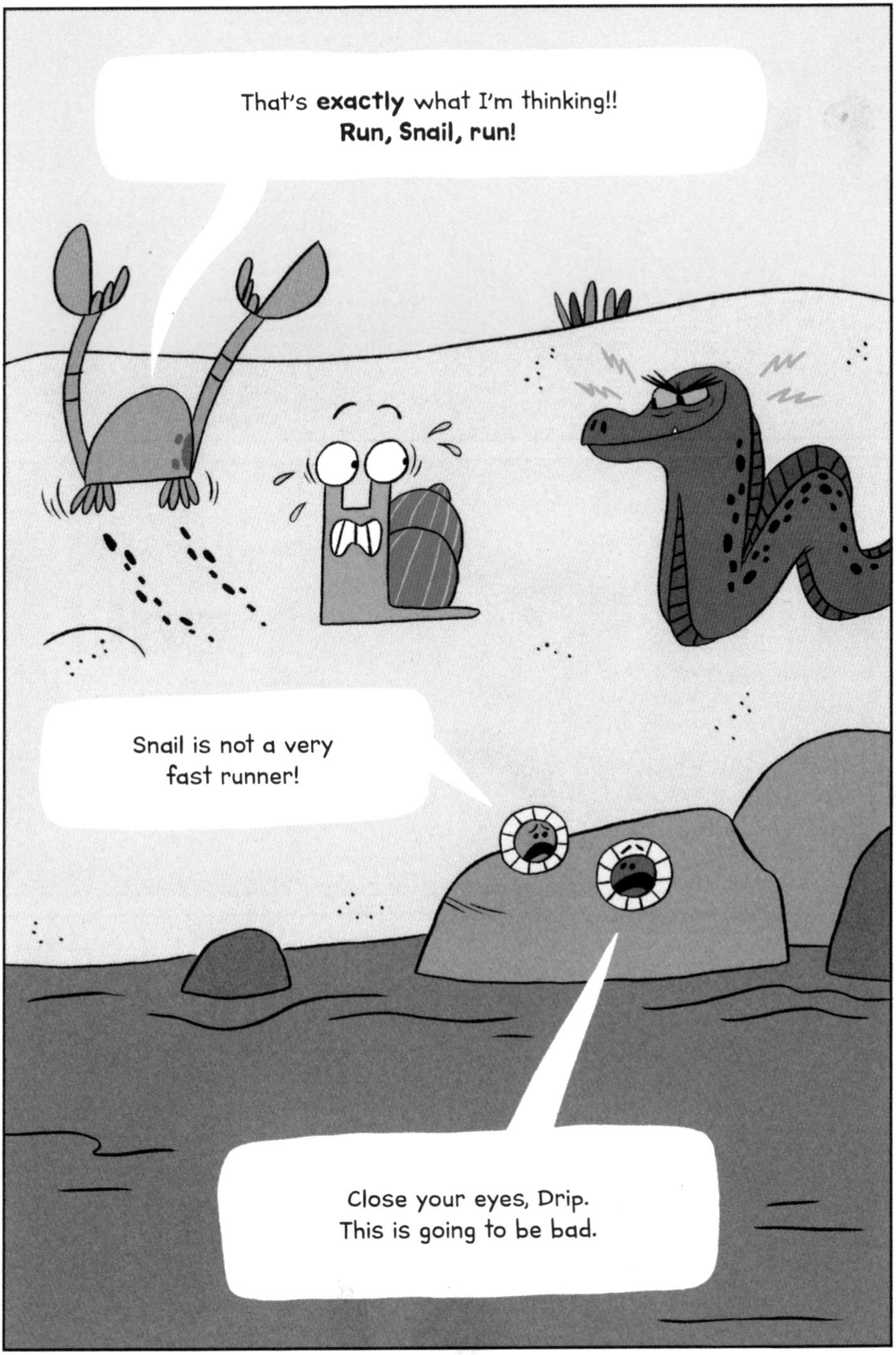
That's **exactly** what I'm thinking!!
Run, Snail, run!
Snail is not a very fast runner!
Close your eyes, Drip. This is going to be bad.

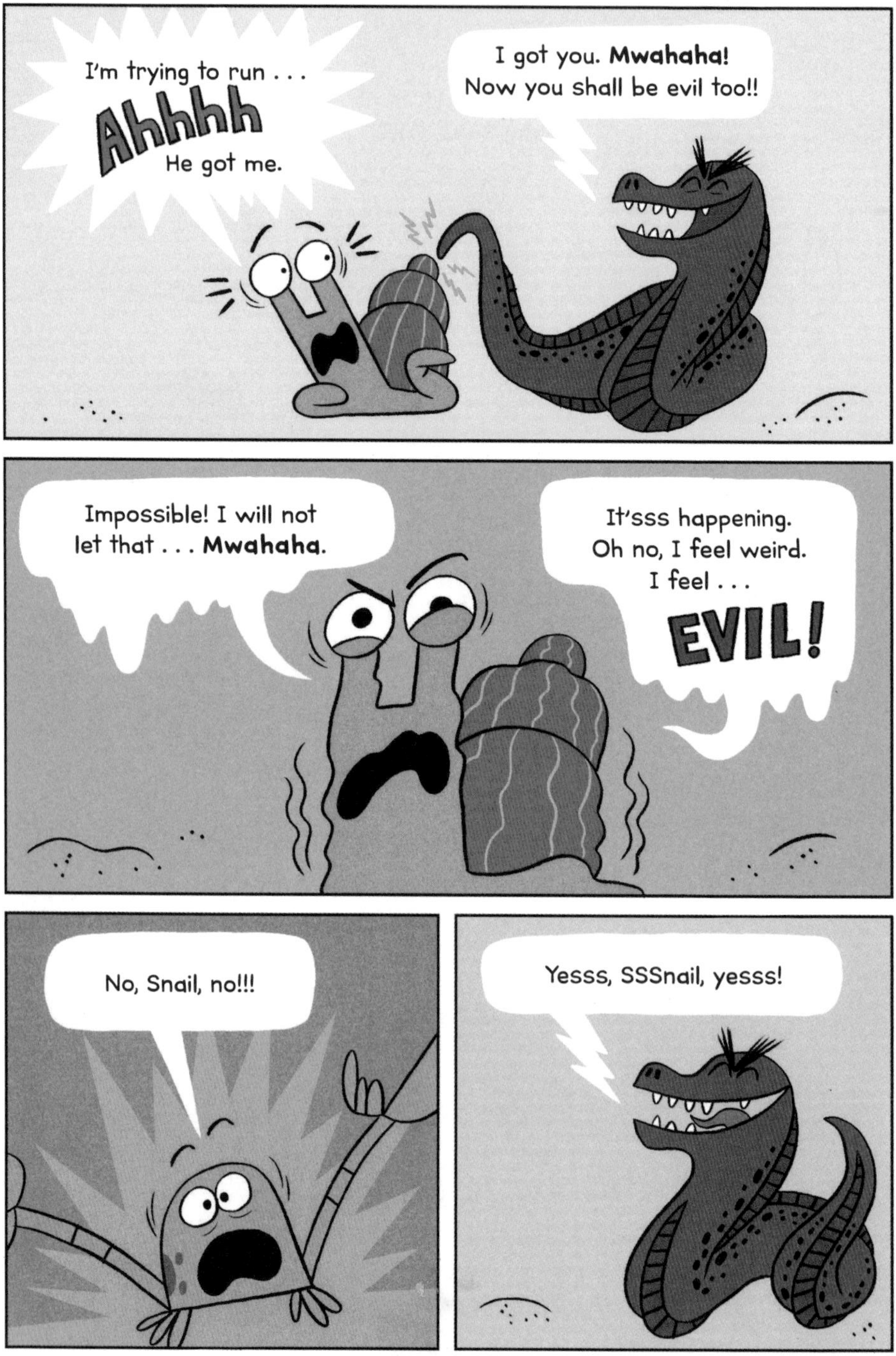
I'm trying to run . . .
Ahhhh
He got me.
I got you. **Mwahaha!** Now you shall be evil too!!
Impossible! I will not let that . . . **Mwahaha**.
It'sss happening. Oh no, I feel weird. I feel . . .
EVIL!
No, Snail, no!!!
Yesss, SSSnail, yesss!

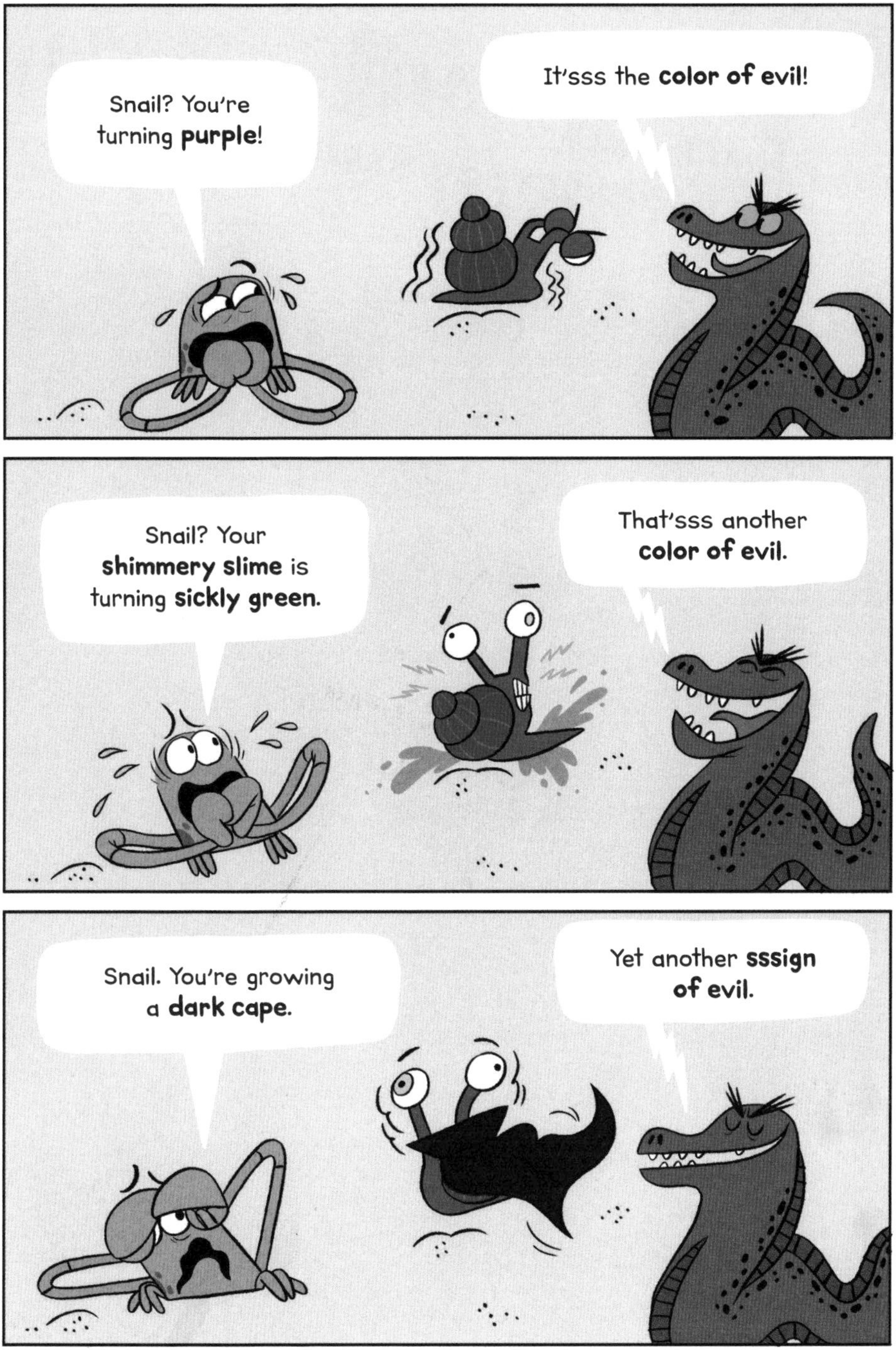
Snail? You're turning **purple**!
It'sss the **color of evil**!
Snail? Your **shimmery slime** is turning **sickly green**.
That'sss another **color of evil**.
Snail. You're growing a **dark cape**.
Yet another **sssign of evil**.

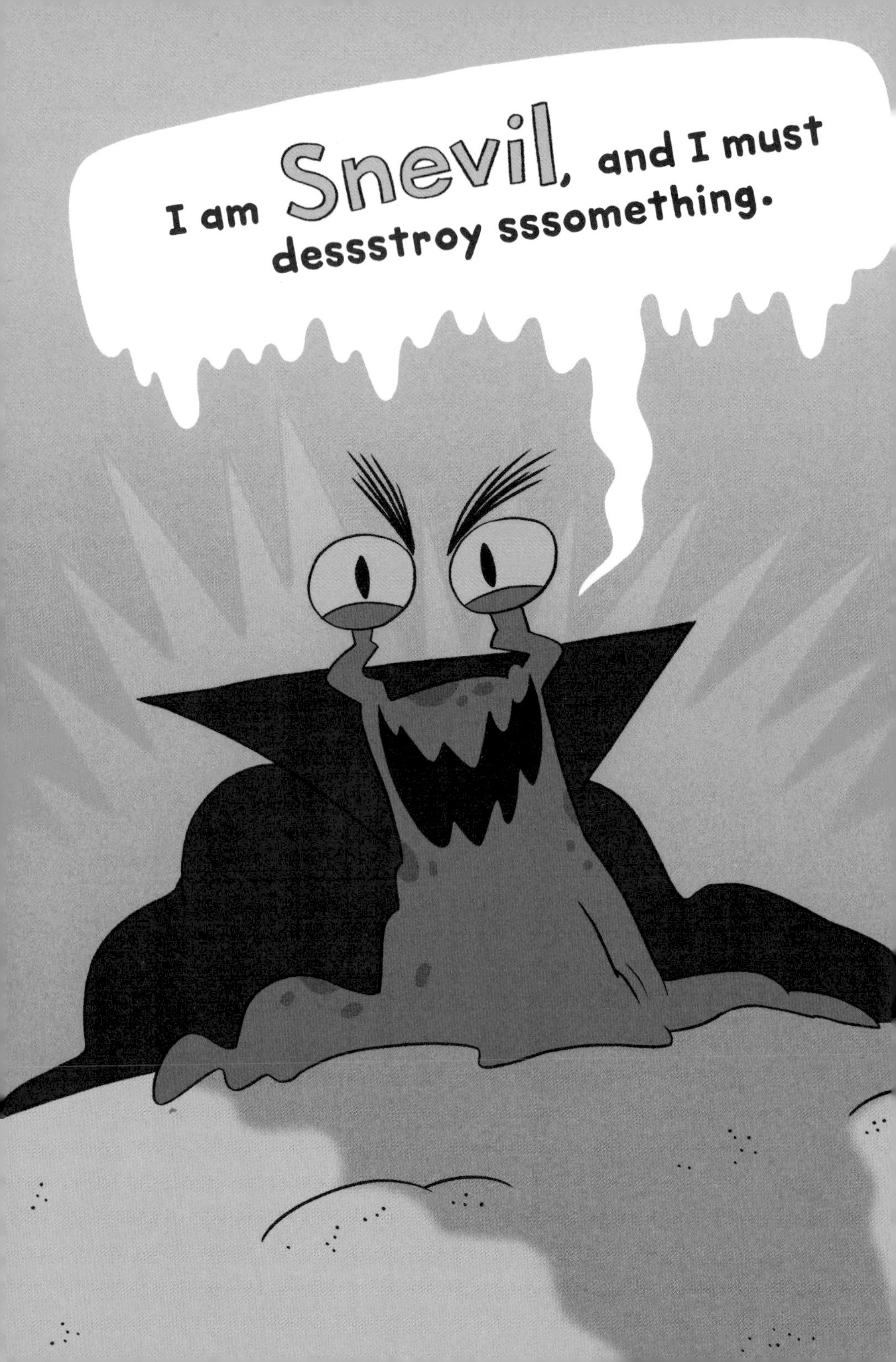
I am Snevil, and I must dessstroy sssomething.

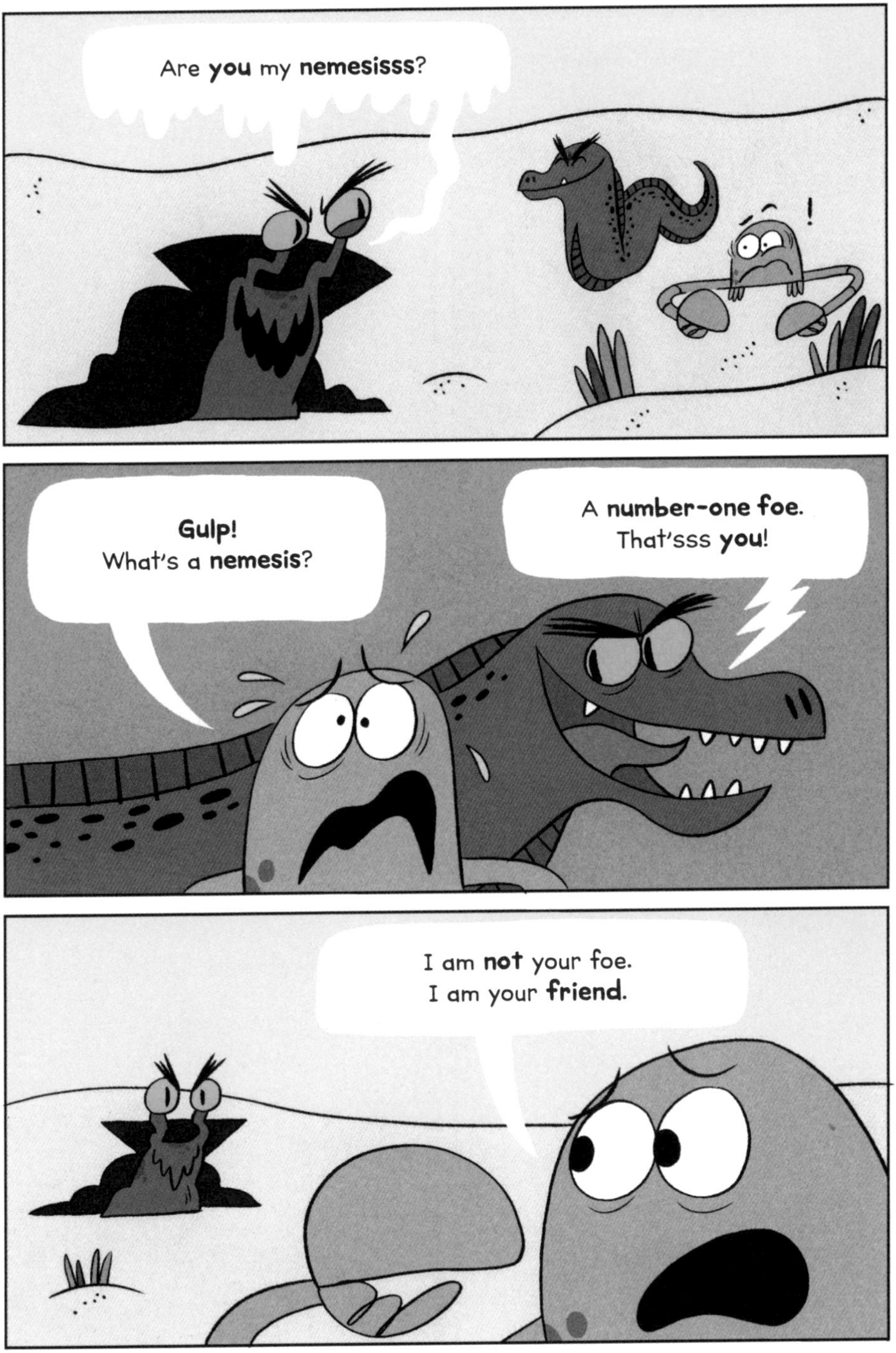
Are **you** my **nemesisss**?
!
Gulp! What's a **nemesis**?
A **number-one foe.** That'sss **you**!
I am **not** your foe. I am your **friend**.

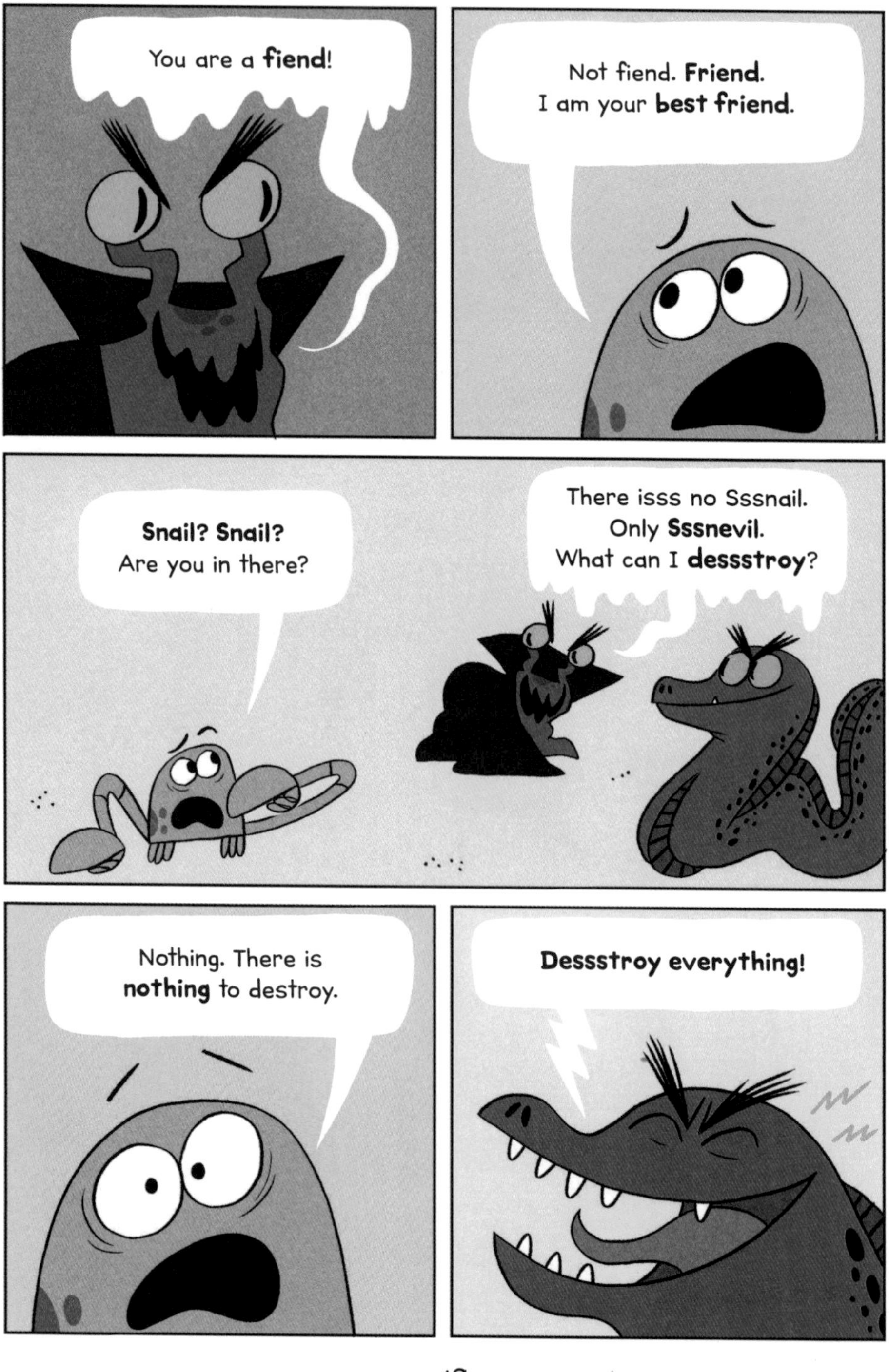
You are a fiend!
Not fiend. Friend. I am your best friend.
Snail? Snail? Are you in there?
There isss no Sssnail. Only Sssnevil. What can I desssstroy?
Nothing. There is nothing to destroy.
Dessstroy everything!

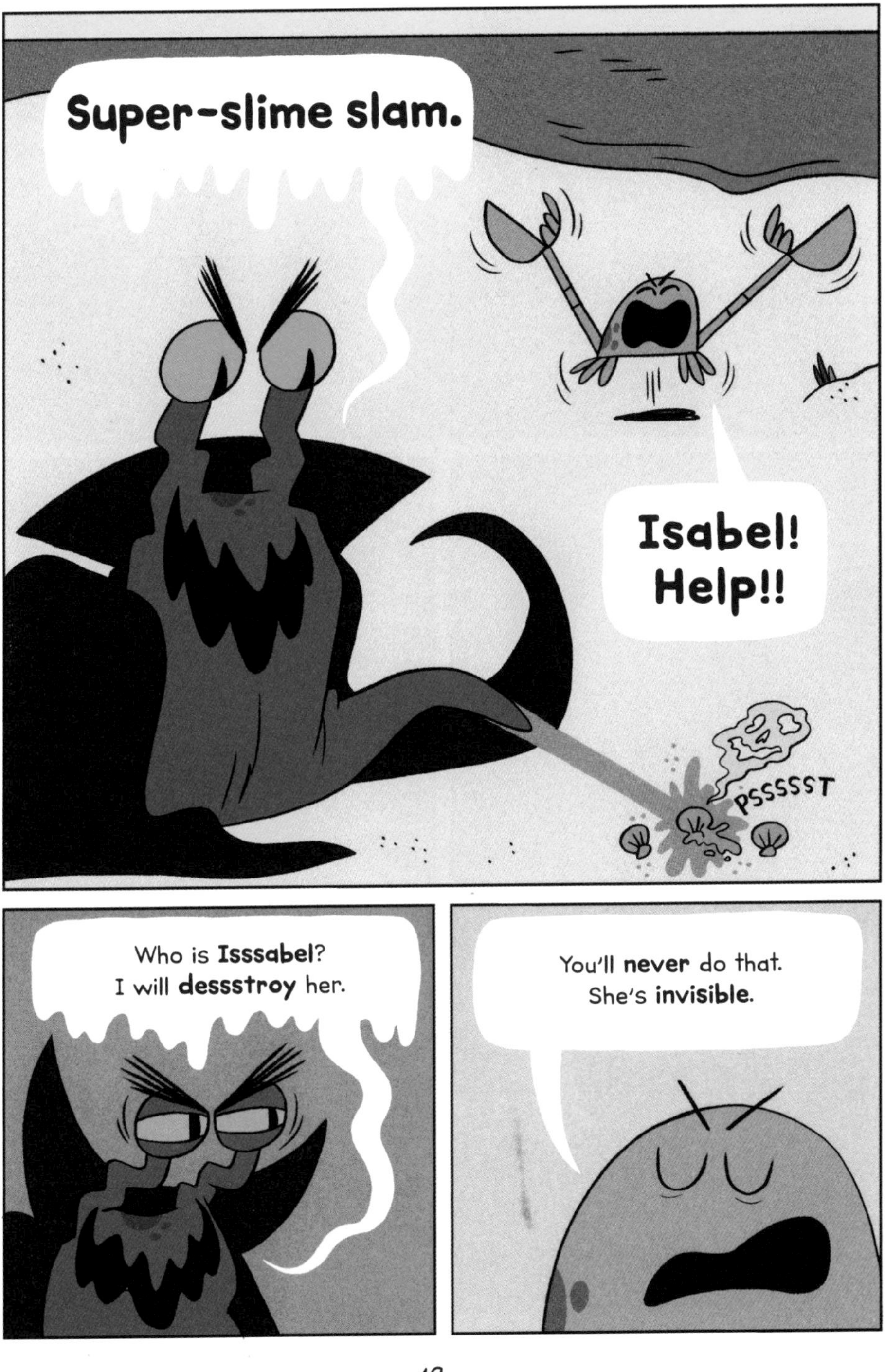
Super-slime slam.
Isabel! Help!!
PSSSSST
Who is **Isssabel**? I will **dessstroy** her.
You'll **never** do that. She's **invisible**.

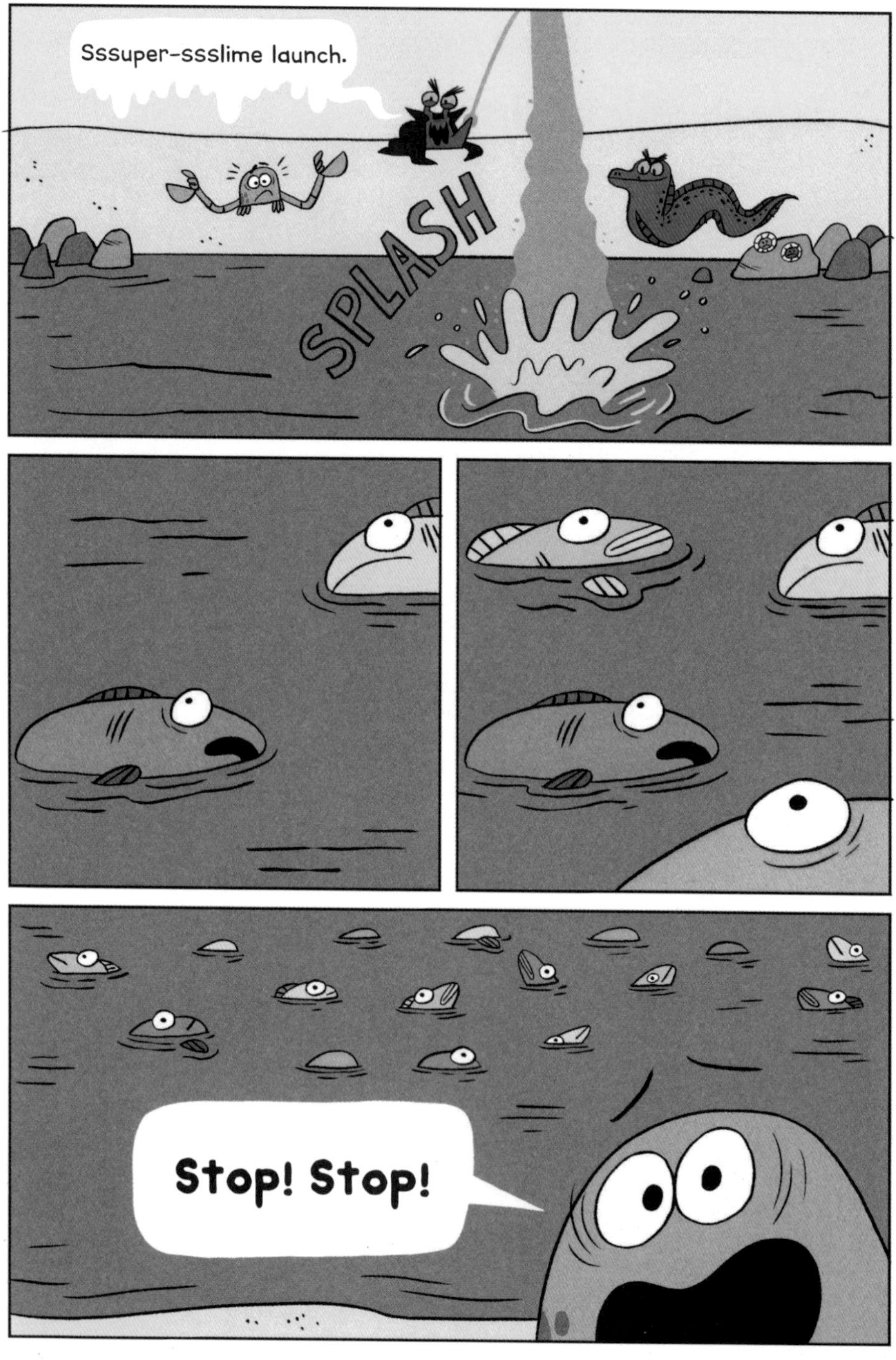
Sssuper-ssslime launch.
SPLASH
Stop! Stop!

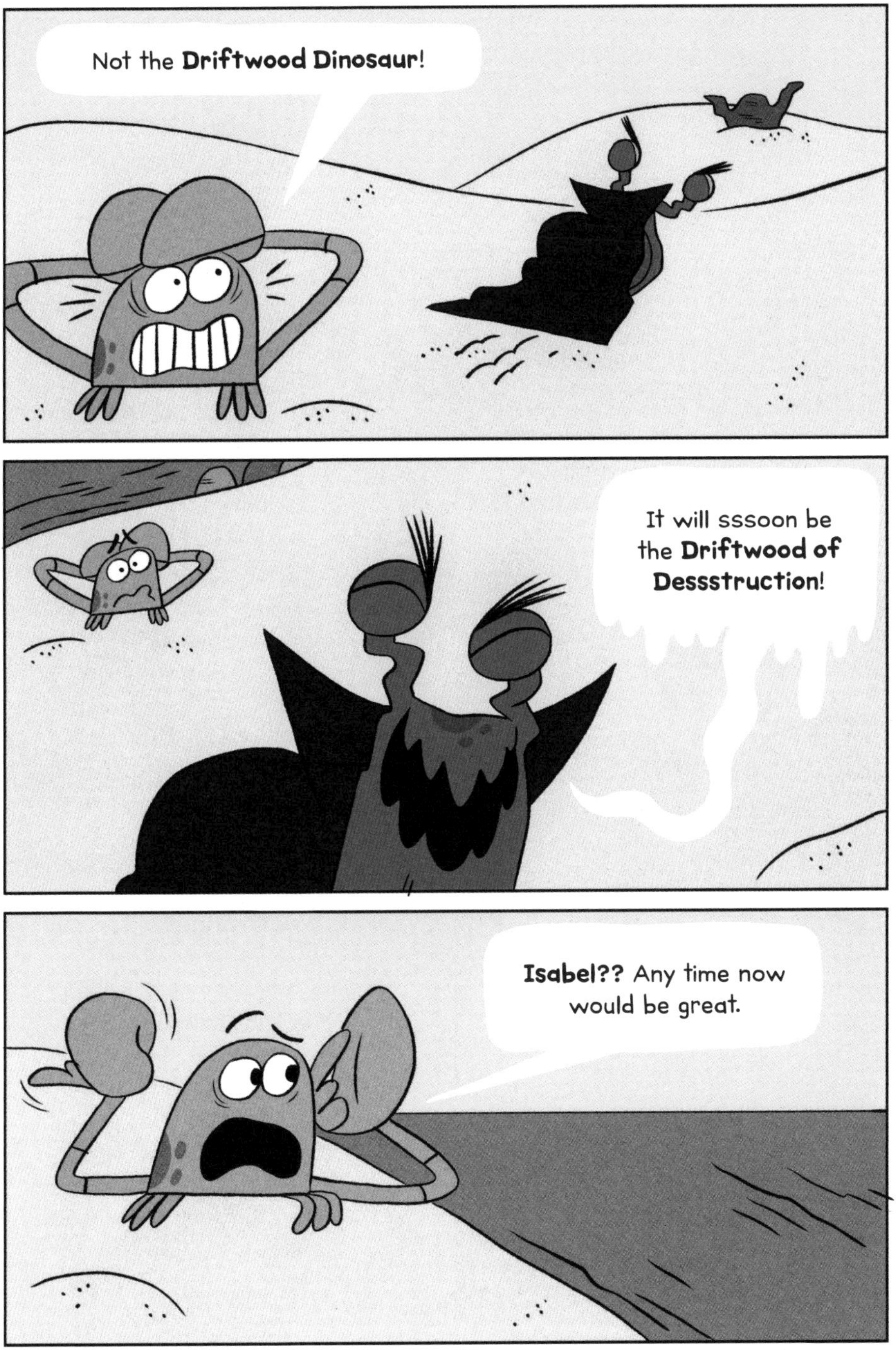
Not the **Driftwood Dinosaur**!
It will sssoon be the **Driftwood of Dessstruction**!
Isabel?? Any time now would be great.

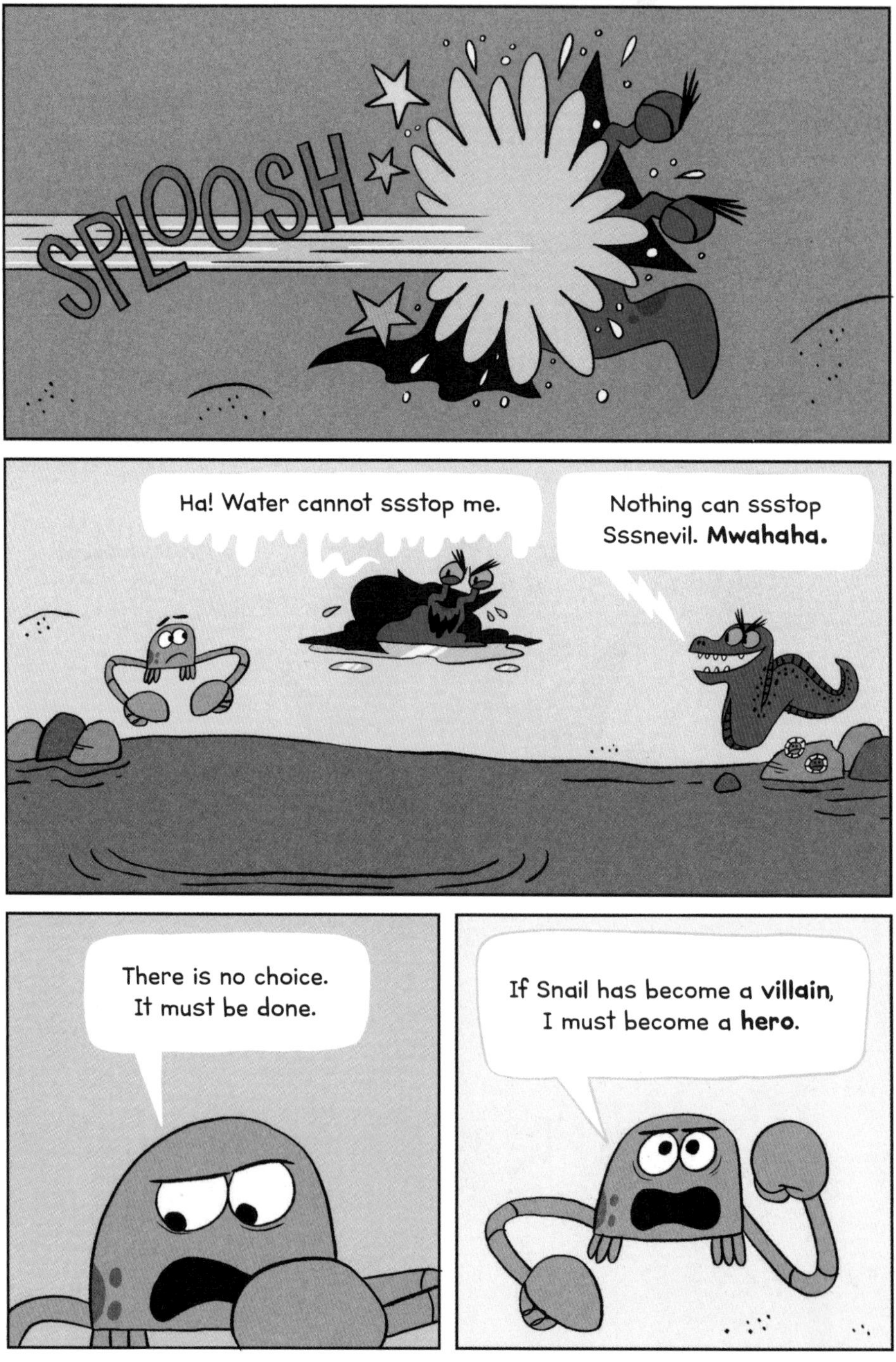
SPLOOSH
Ha! Water cannot ssstop me.
Nothing can ssstop Sssnevil. **Mwahaha.**
There is no choice. It must be done.
If Snail has become a **villain**, I must become a **hero**.

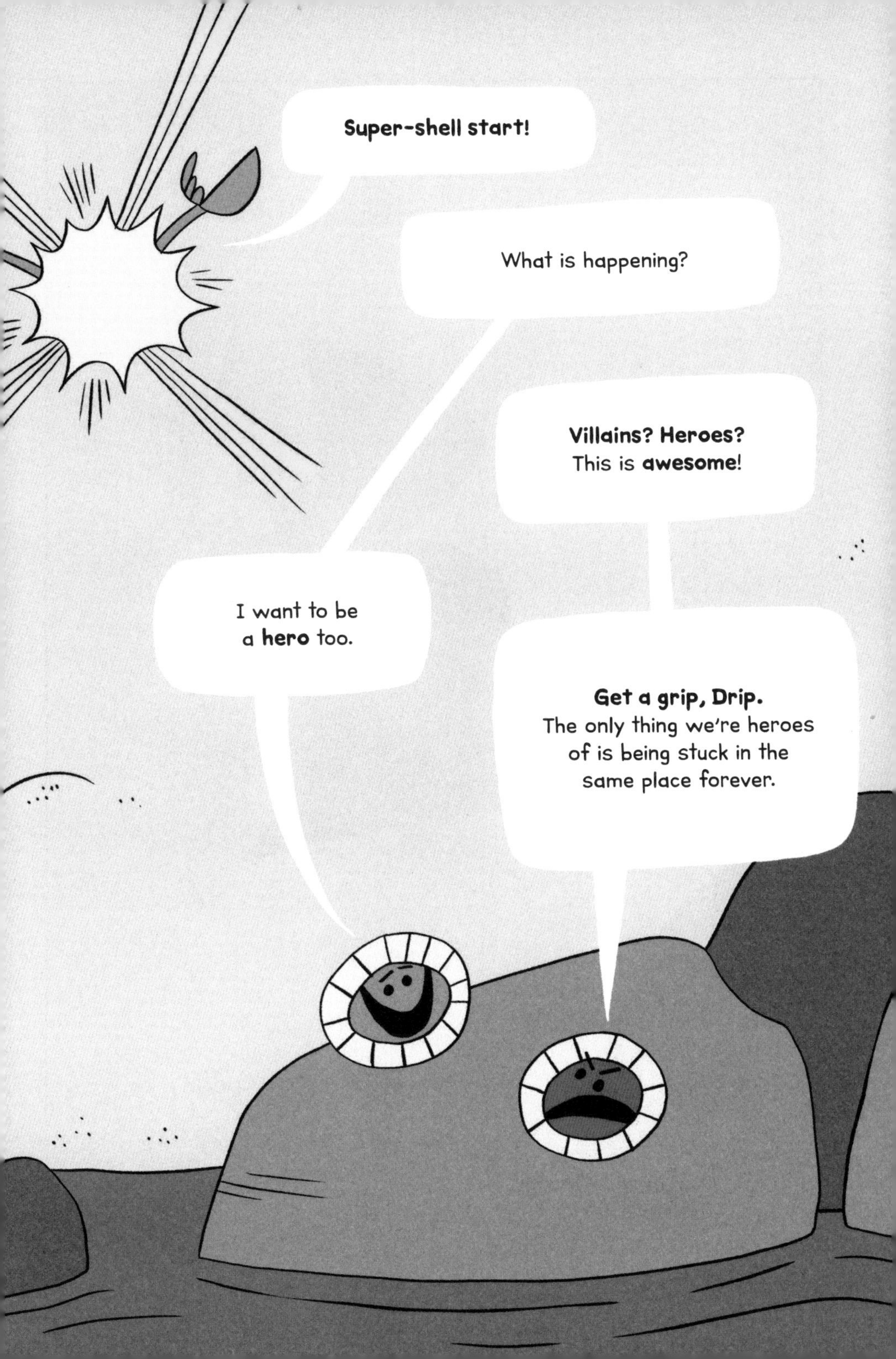
Super-shell start!
What is happening?
Villains? Heroes? This is awesome!
I want to be a hero too.
Get a grip, Drip. The only thing we're heroes of is being stuck in the same place forever.

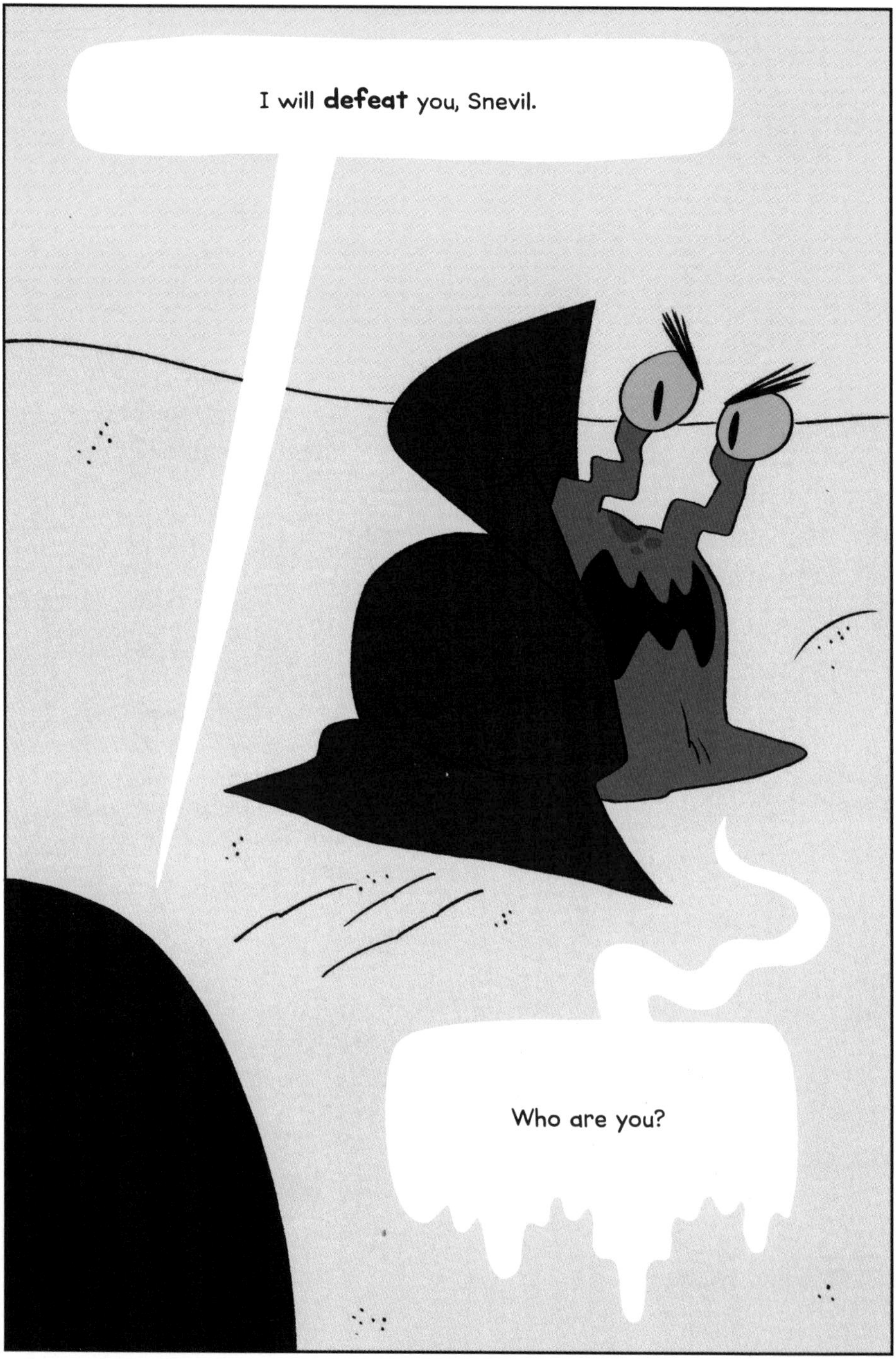
I will **defeat** you, Snevil.
Who are you?

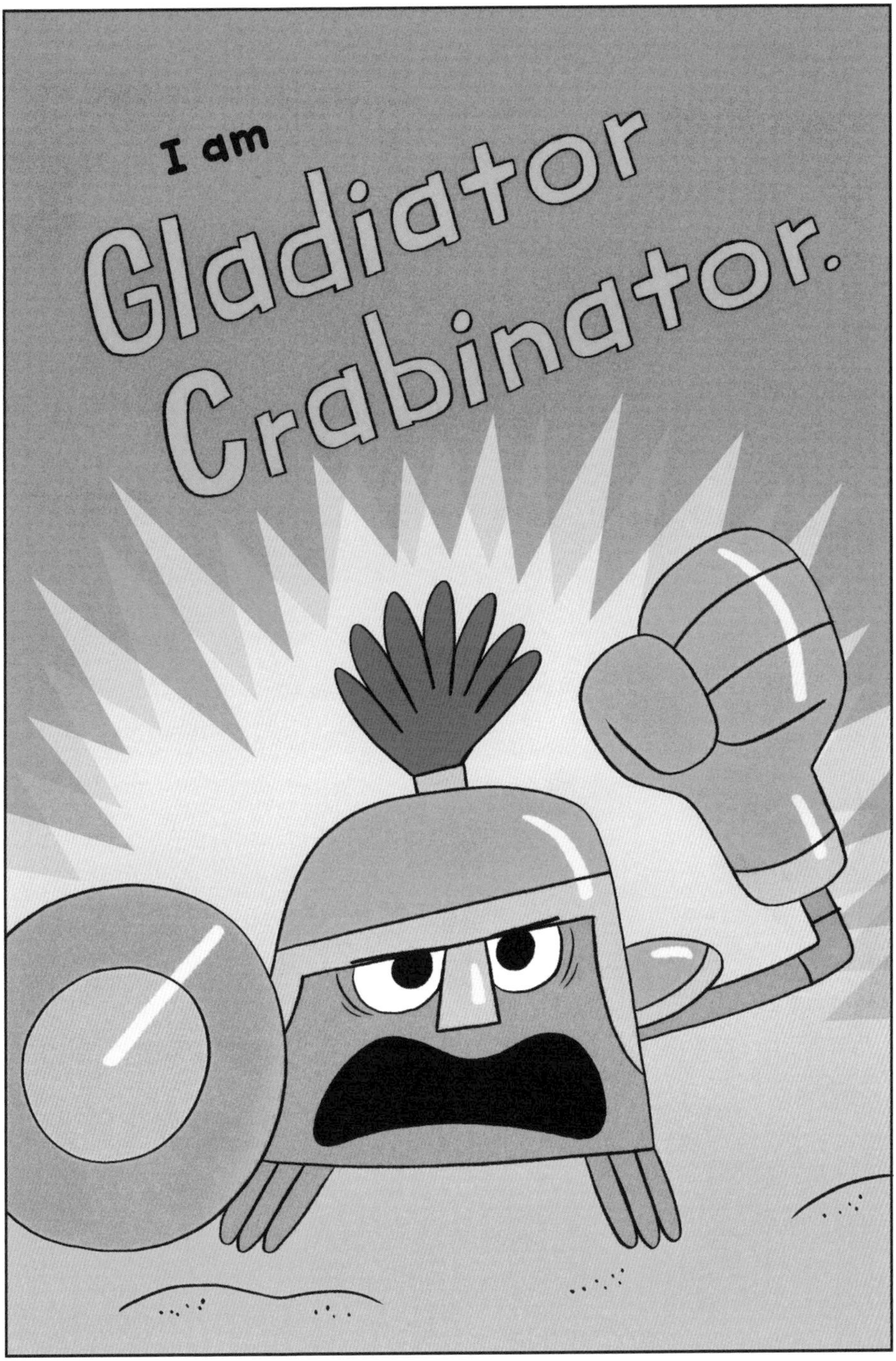
I am
Gladiator Crabinator.

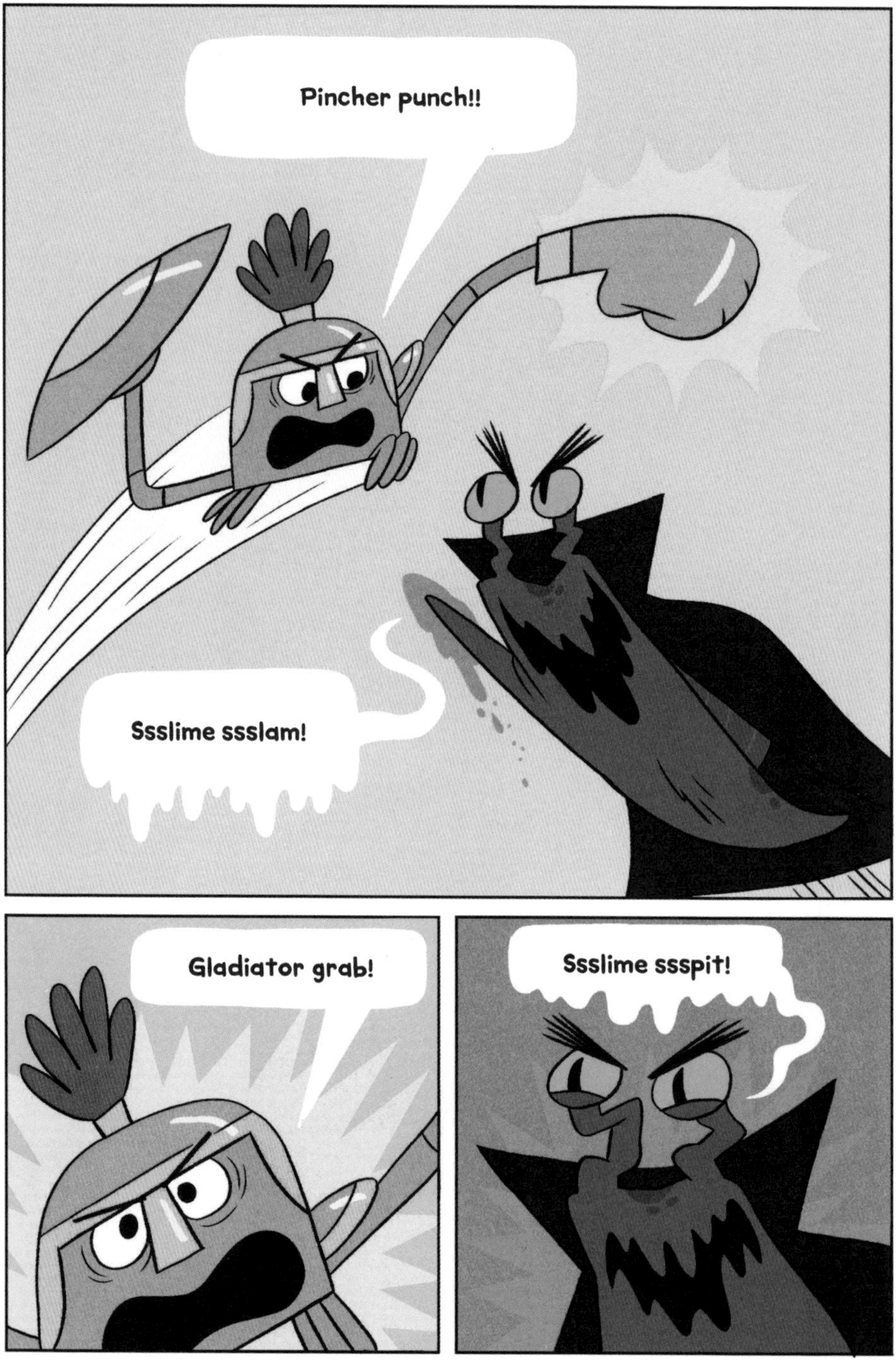
Pincher punch!!
Ssslime ssslam!
Gladiator grab!
Ssslime ssspit!

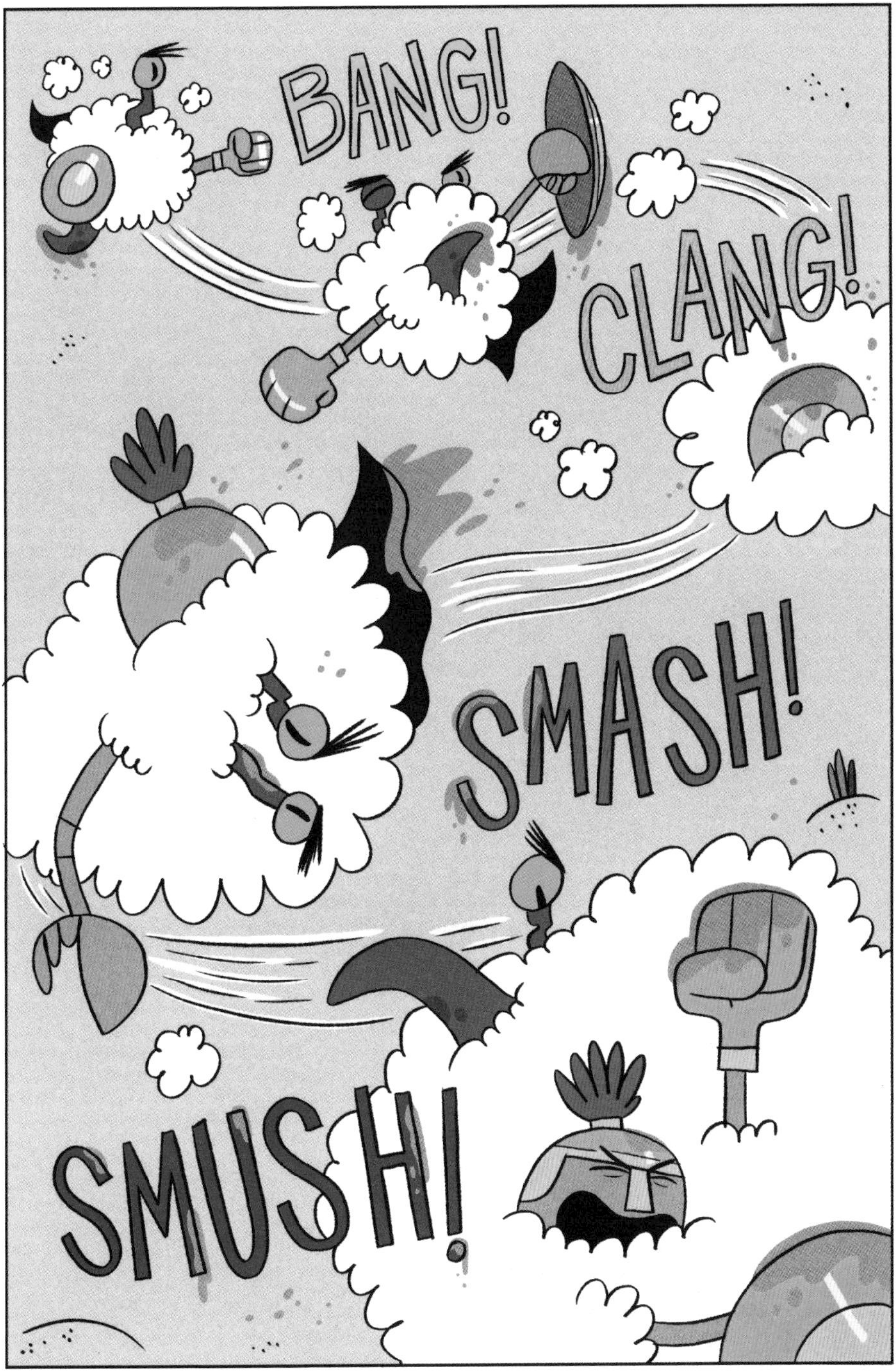
BANG!
CLANG!
SMASH!
SMUSH!

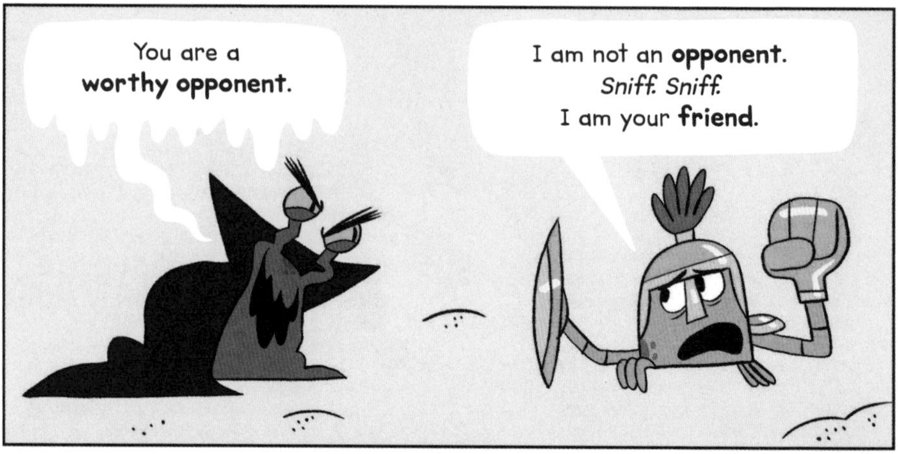
You are a **worthy opponent.**
I am not an **opponent.** *Sniff. Sniff.* I am your **friend.**

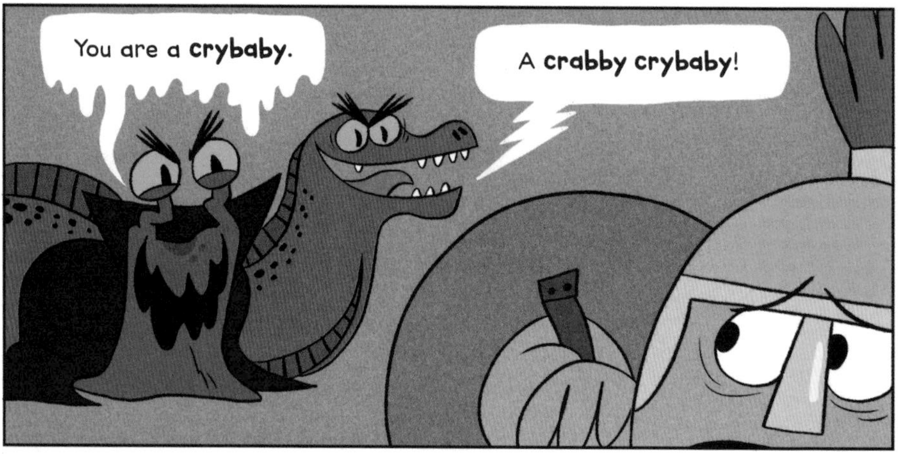
You are a **crybaby.**
A **crabby crybaby!**

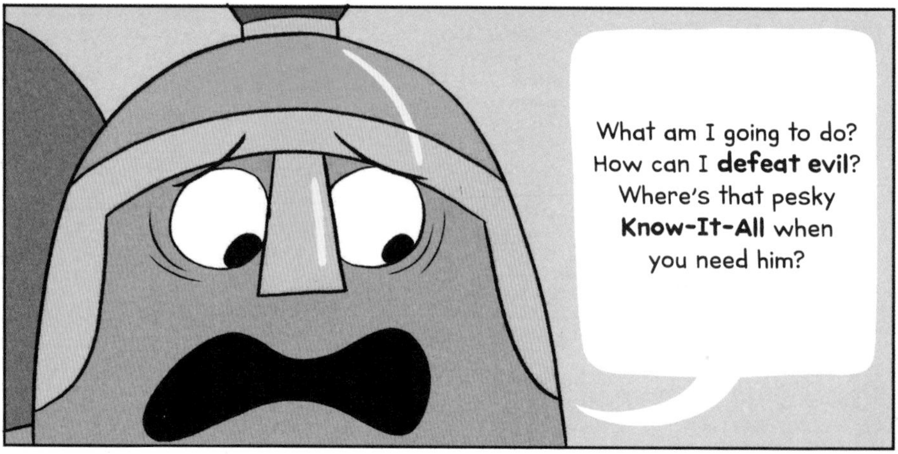
What am I going to do? How can I **defeat evil**? Where's that pesky **Know-It-All** when you need him?

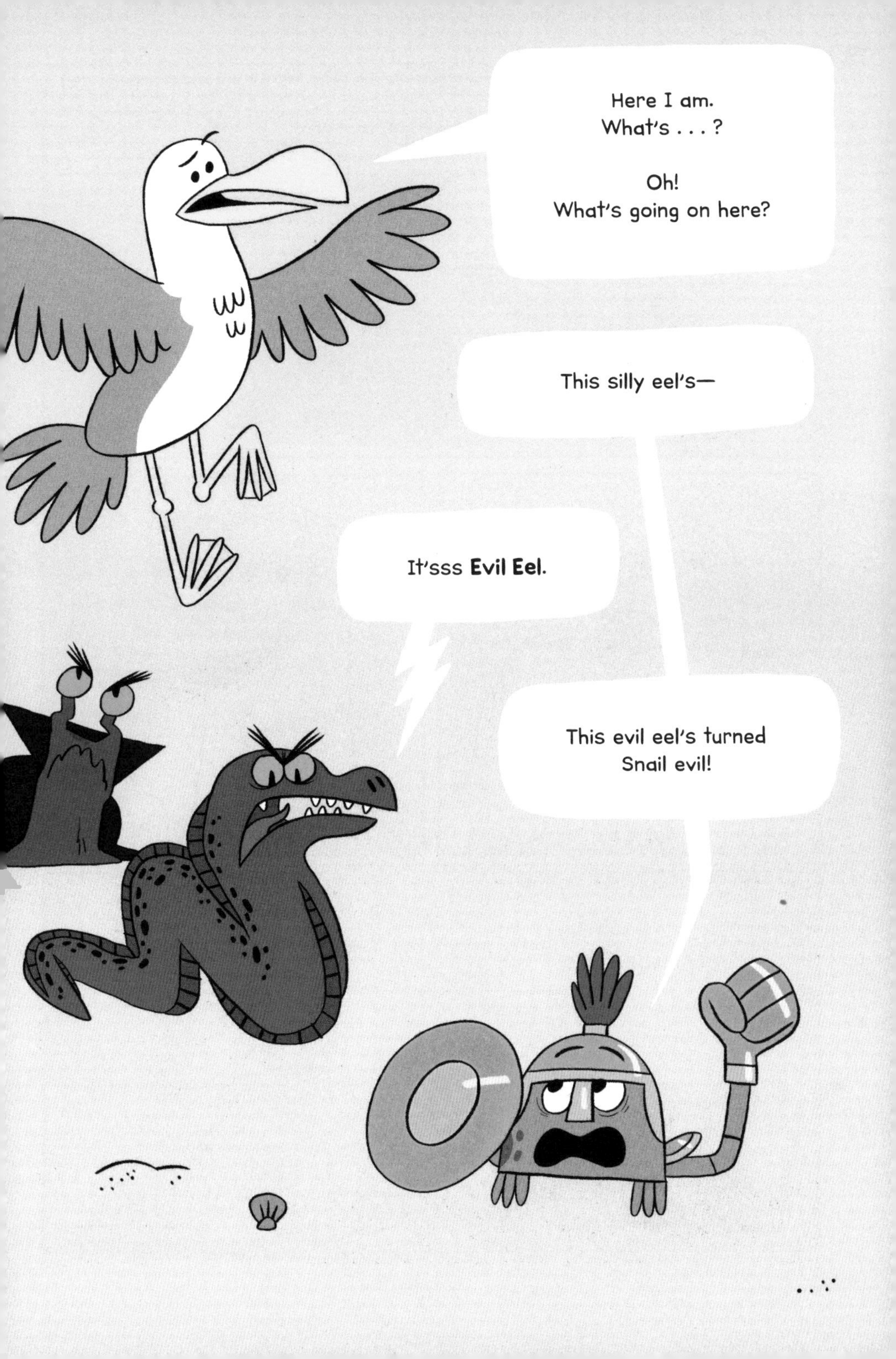
Here I am.
What's . . . ?
Oh!
What's going on here?
This silly eel's—
It'sss **Evil Eel**.
This evil eel's turned
Snail evil!

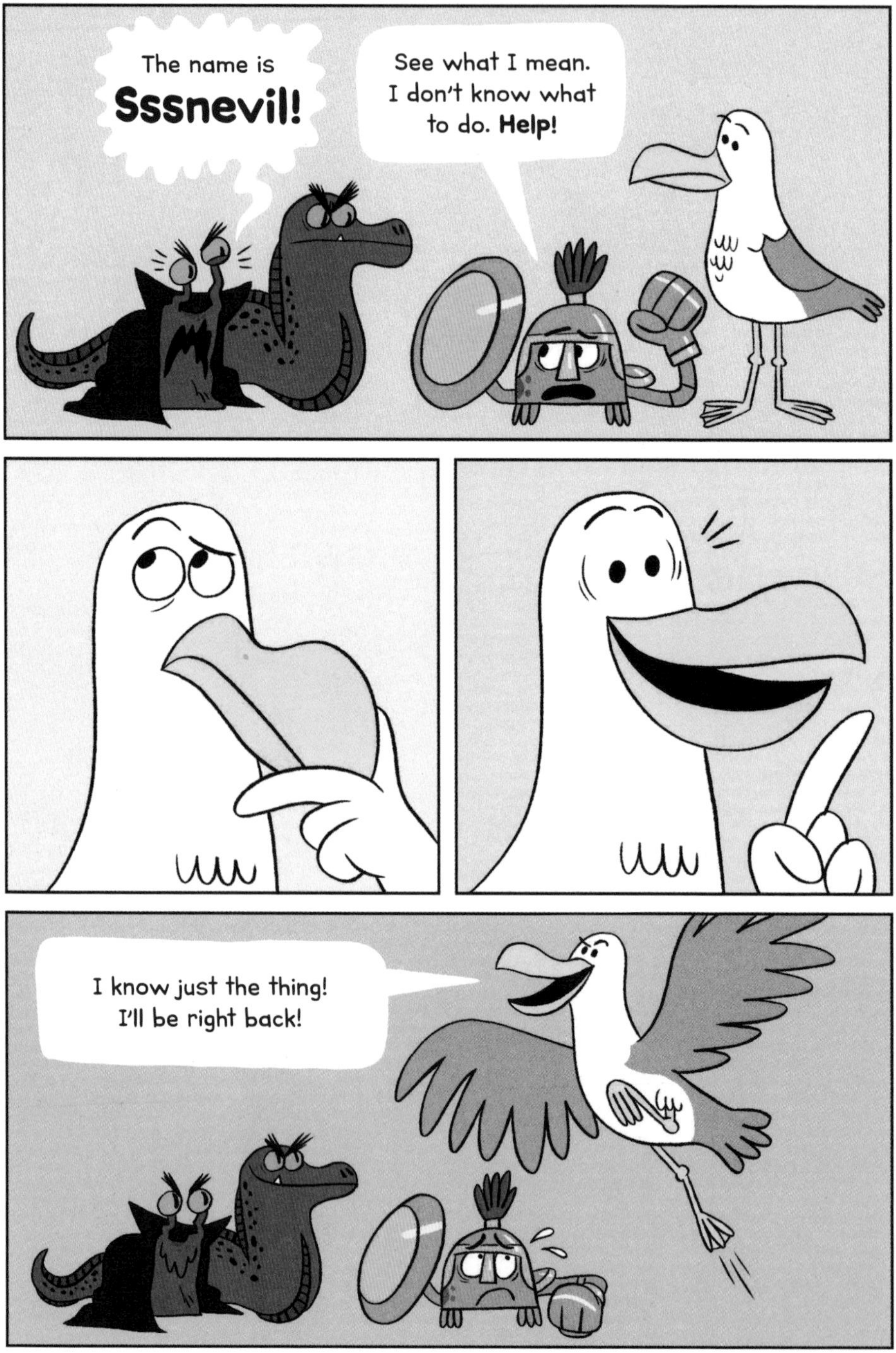
The name is **Sssnevil!**
See what I mean. I don't know what to do. **Help!**
I know just the thing! I'll be right back!

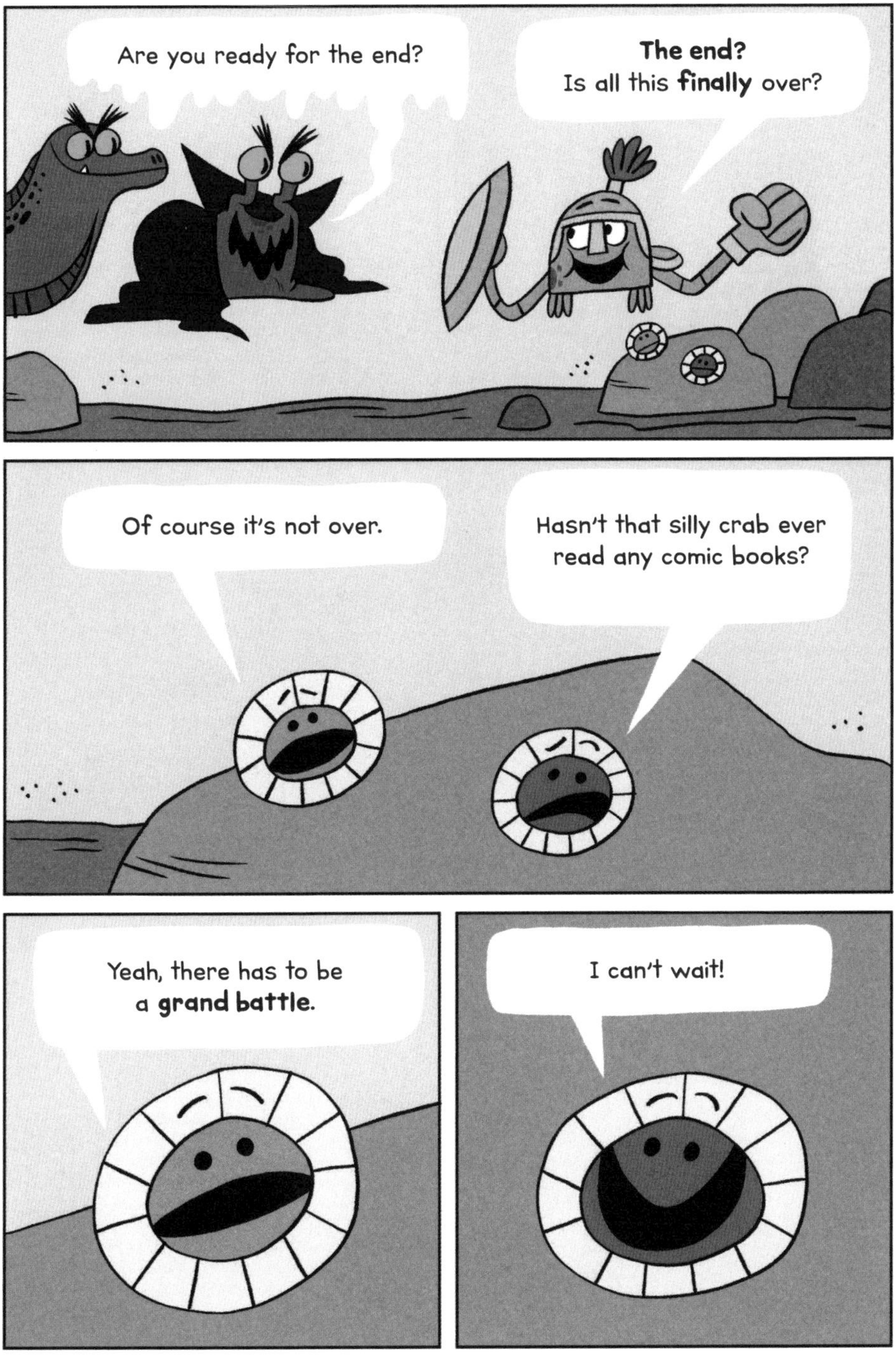
Are you ready for the end?
The end? Is all this **finally** over?
Of course it's not over.
Hasn't that silly crab ever read any comic books?
Yeah, there has to be a **grand battle**.
I can't wait!

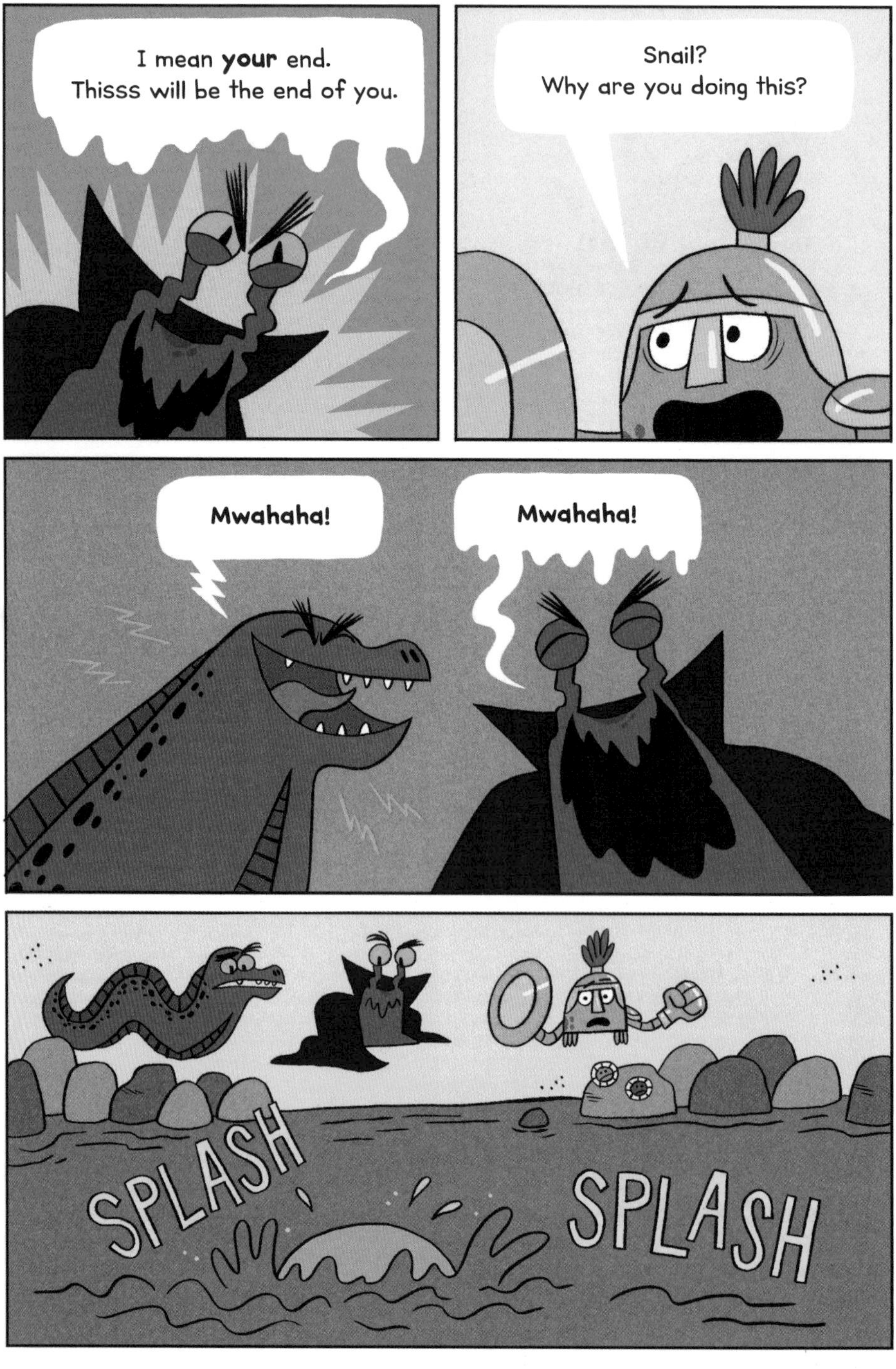
I mean **your** end.
Thisss will be the end of you.
Snail?
Why are you doing this?
Mwahaha!
Mwahaha!
SPLASH
SPLASH

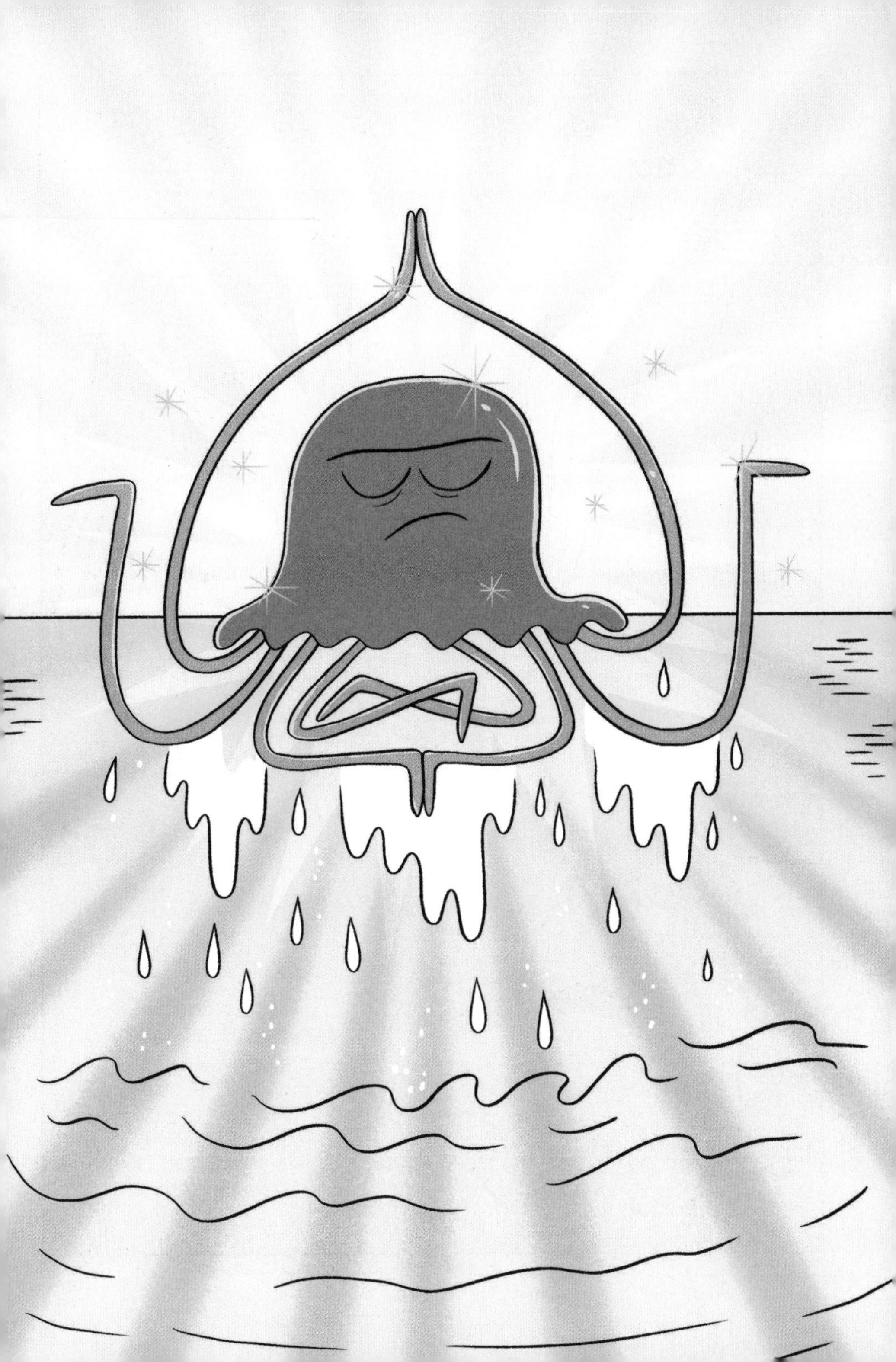

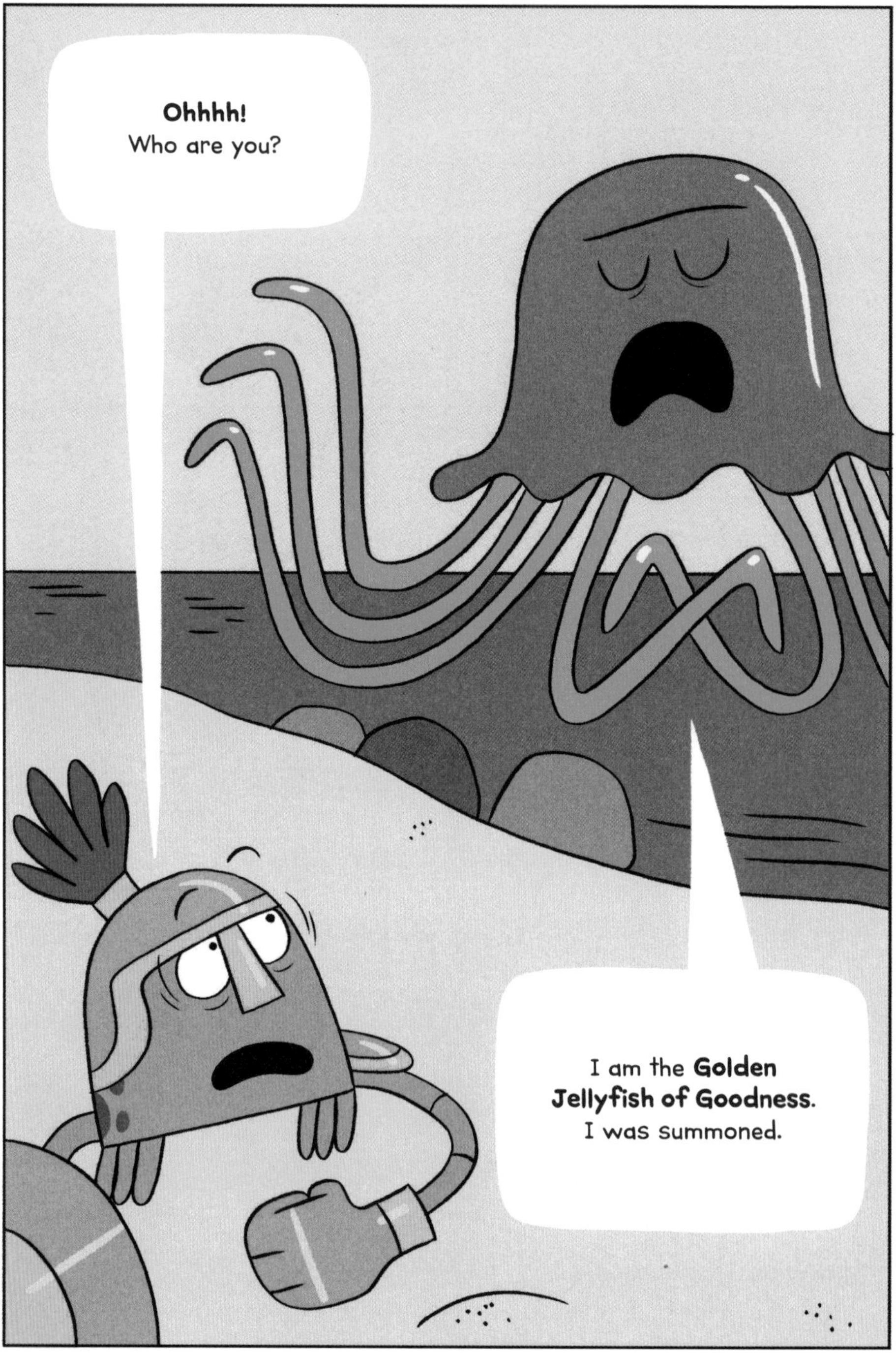
Ohhhh! Who are you?
I am the **Golden Jellyfish of Goodness.** I was summoned.

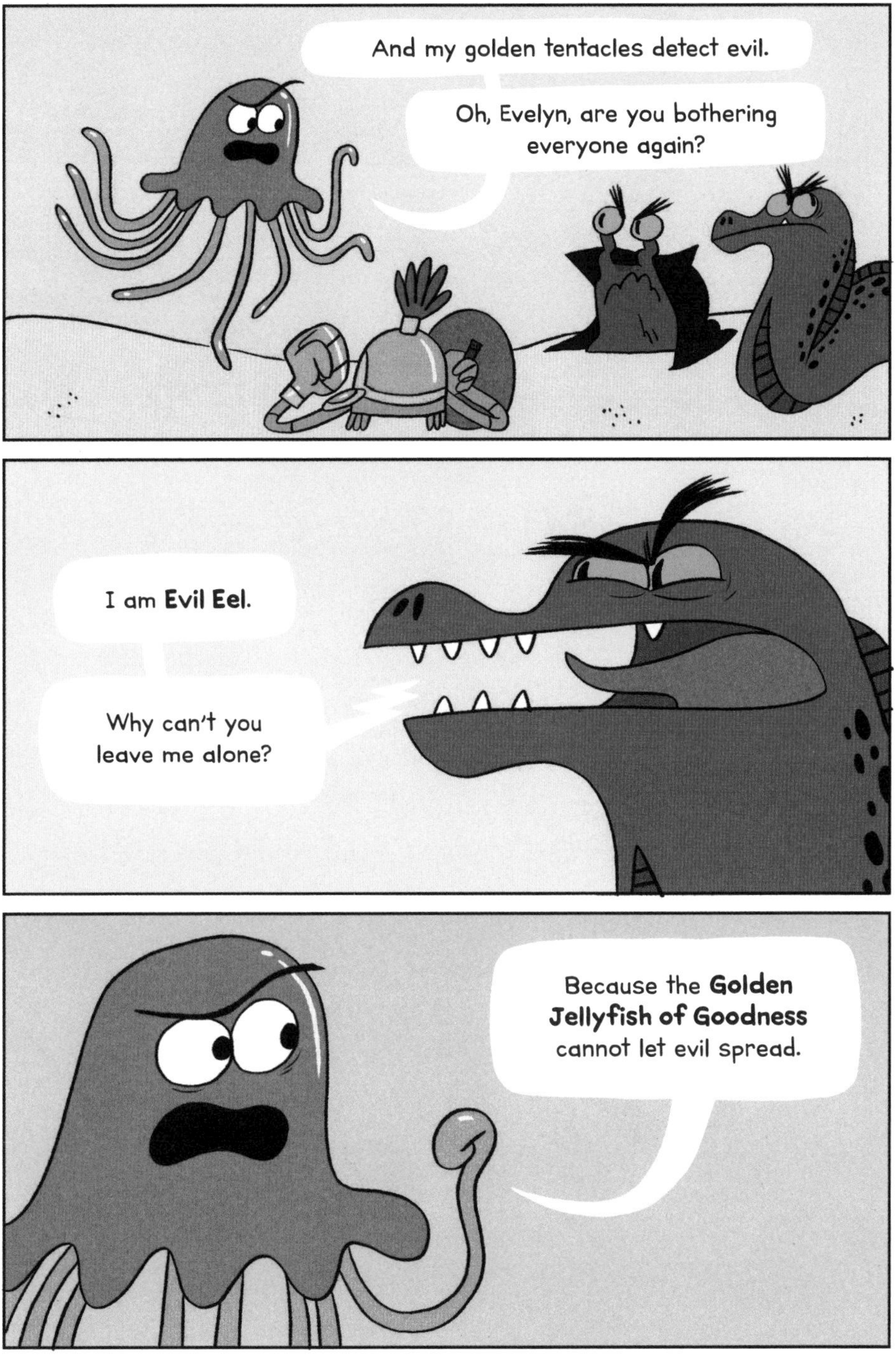
And my golden tentacles detect evil.
Oh, Evelyn, are you bothering everyone again?
I am **Evil Eel**.
Why can't you leave me alone?
Because the **Golden Jellyfish of Goodness** cannot let evil spread.

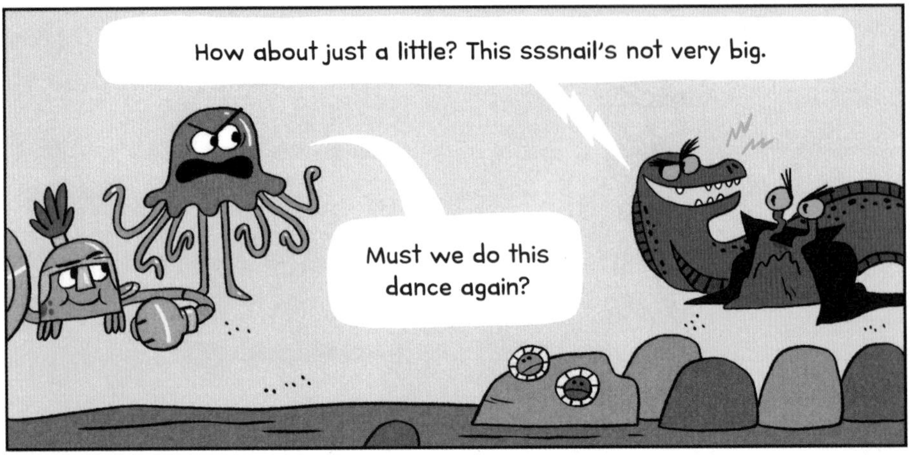
How about just a little? This sssnail's not very big.
Must we do this dance again?

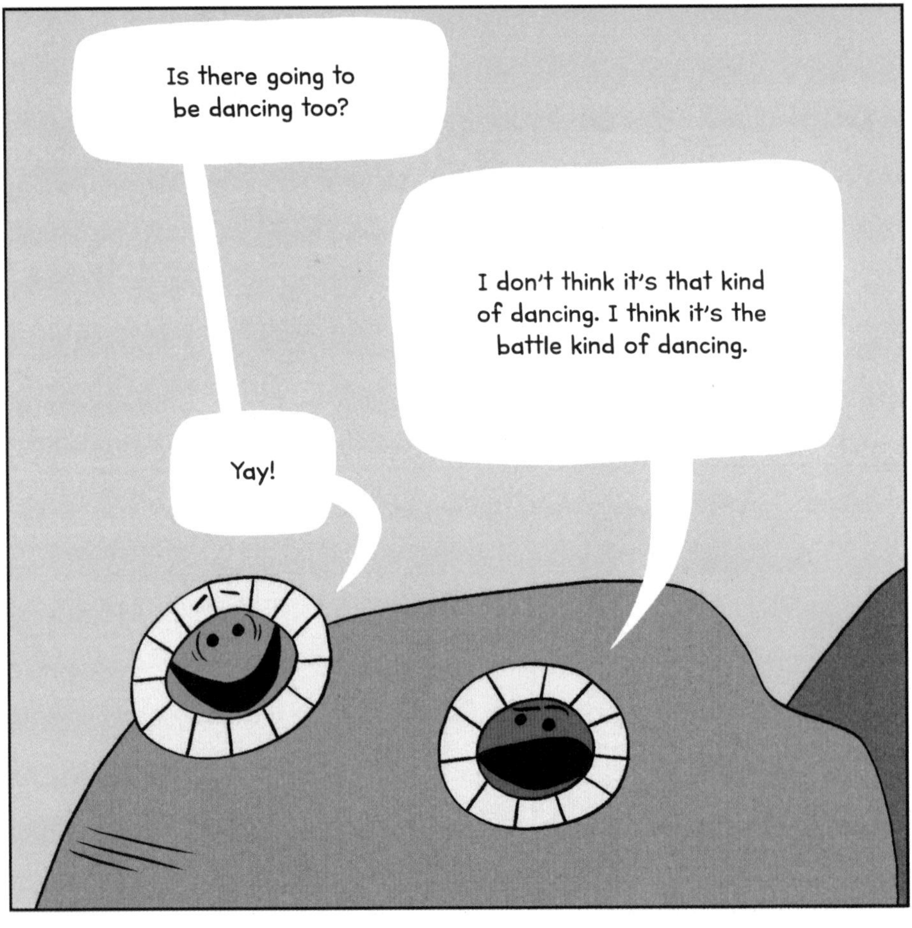
Is there going to be dancing too?
I don't think it's that kind of dancing. I think it's the battle kind of dancing.
Yay!

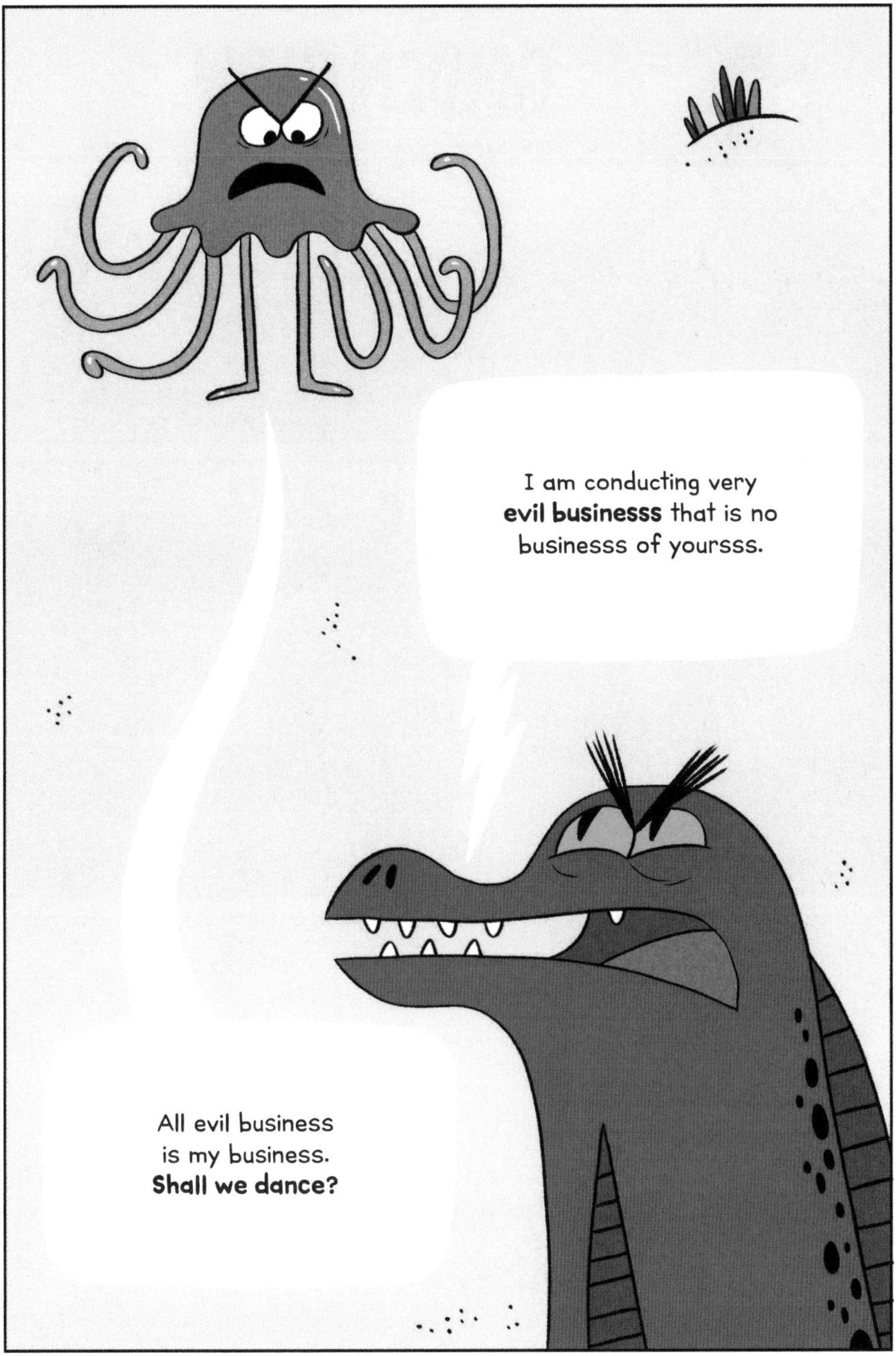
I am conducting very **evil businesss** that is no businesss of yoursss.
All evil business is my business. **Shall we dance?**

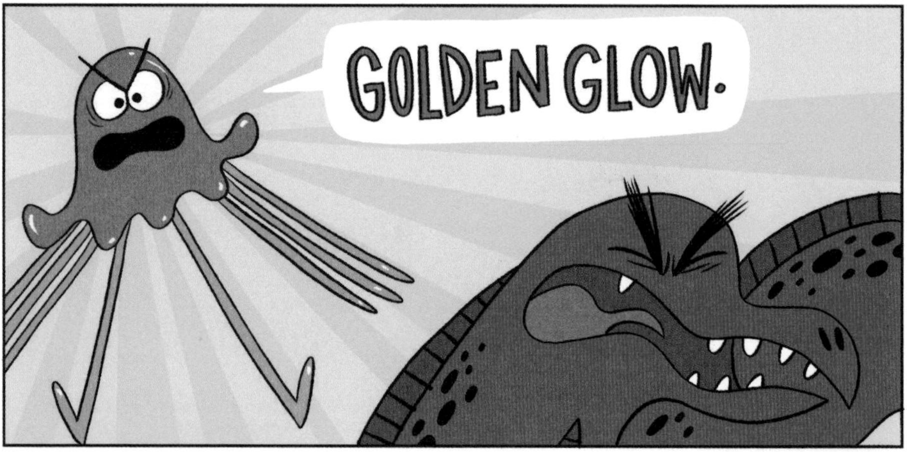
GOLDEN GLOW.

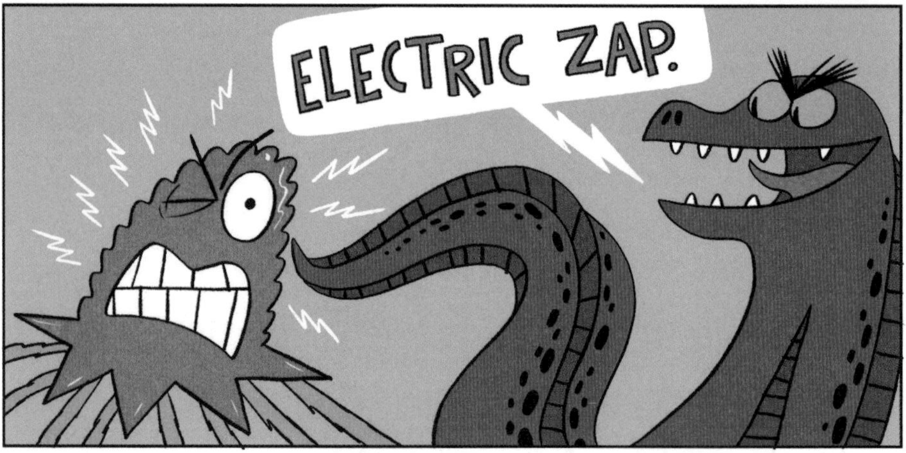
ELECTRIC ZAP.

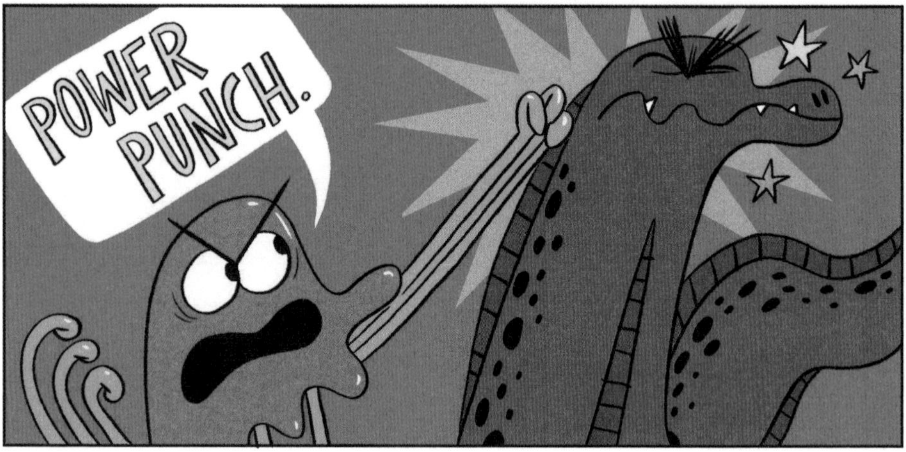
POWER PUNCH.

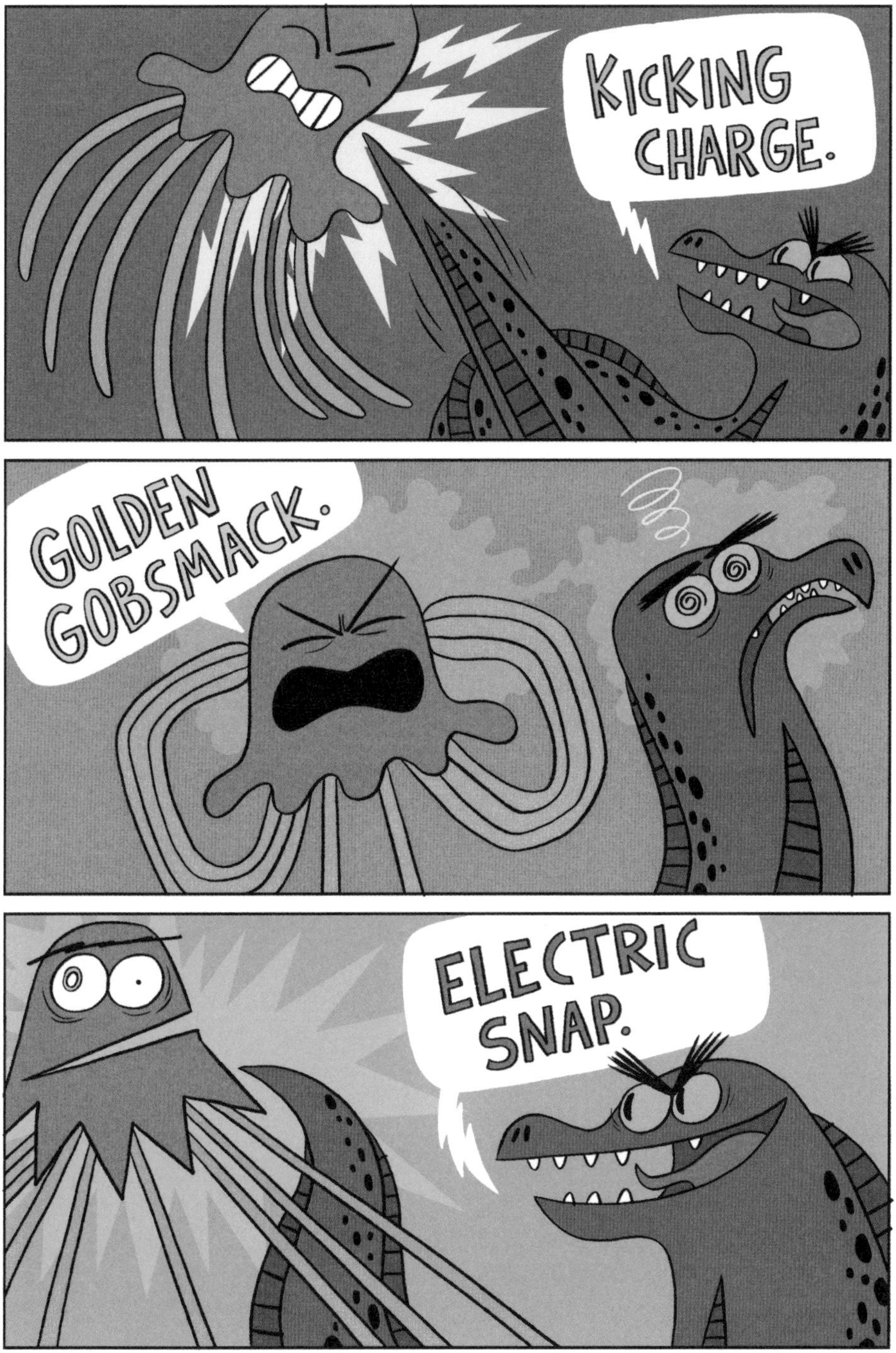
KICKING CHARGE.
GOLDEN GOBSMACK.
ELECTRIC SNAP.

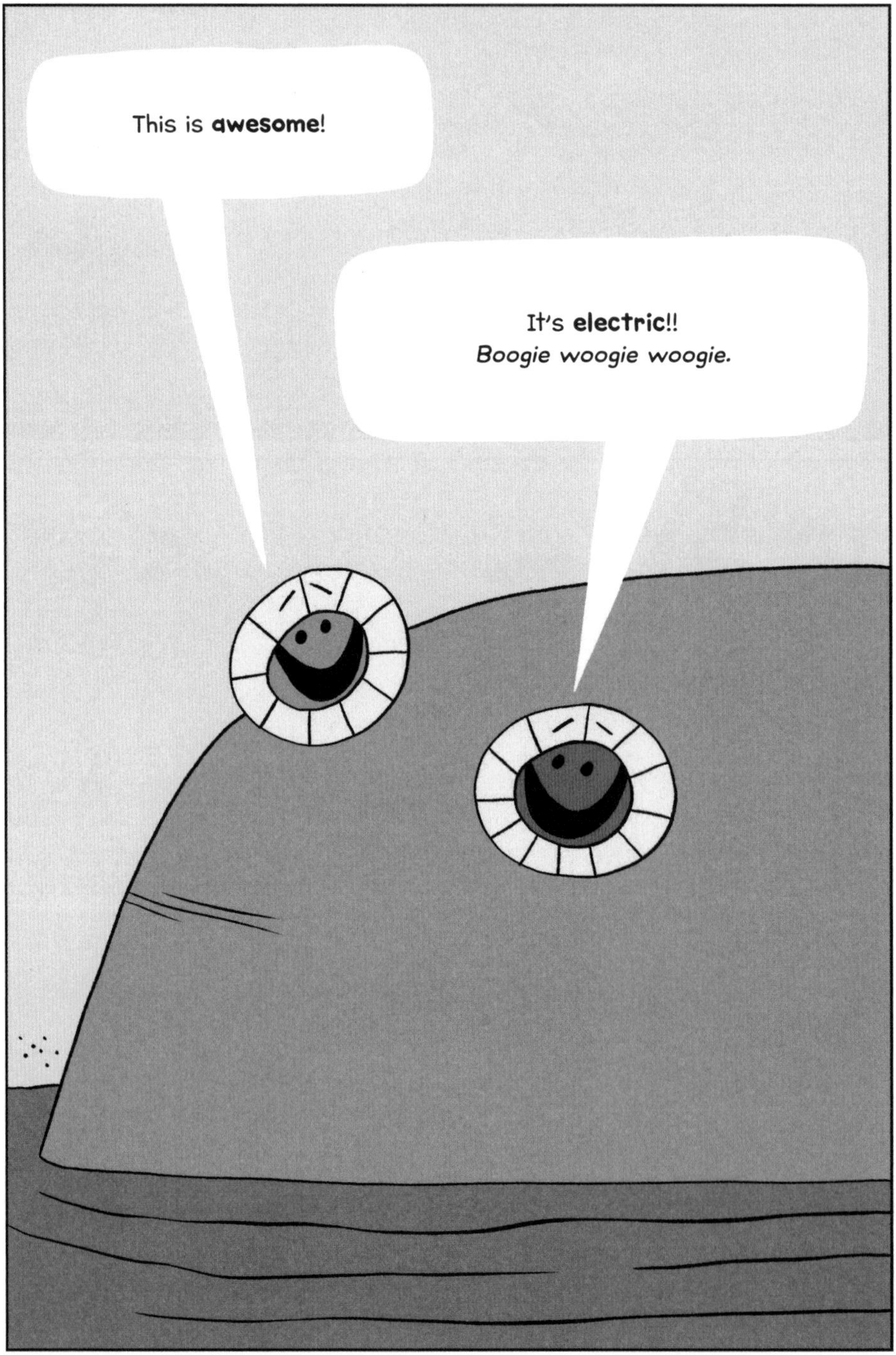
This is **awesome**!
It's **electric**!! *Boogie woogie woogie.*

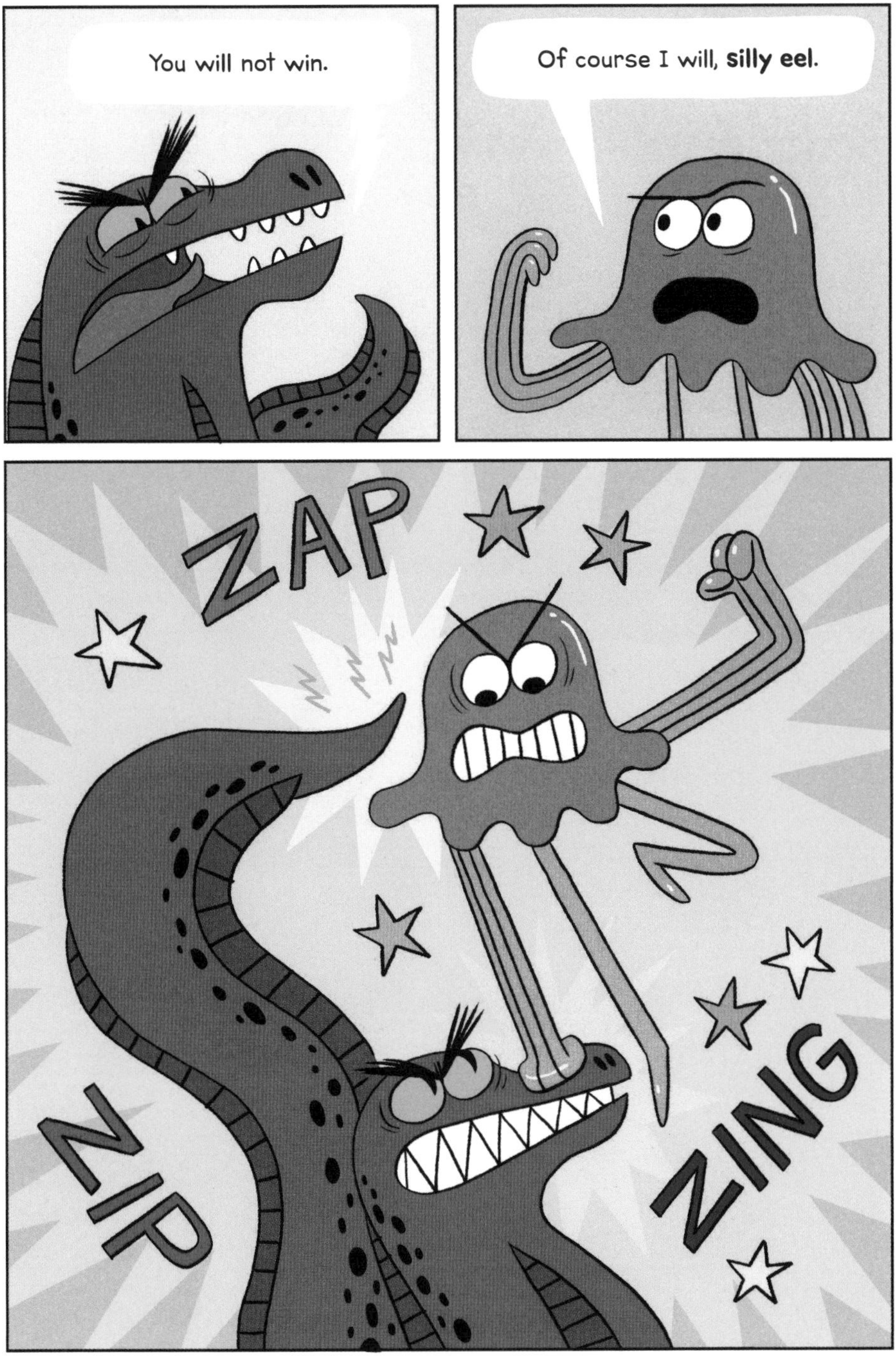
You will not win.
Of course I will, **silly eel**.
ZAP
ZIP
ZING

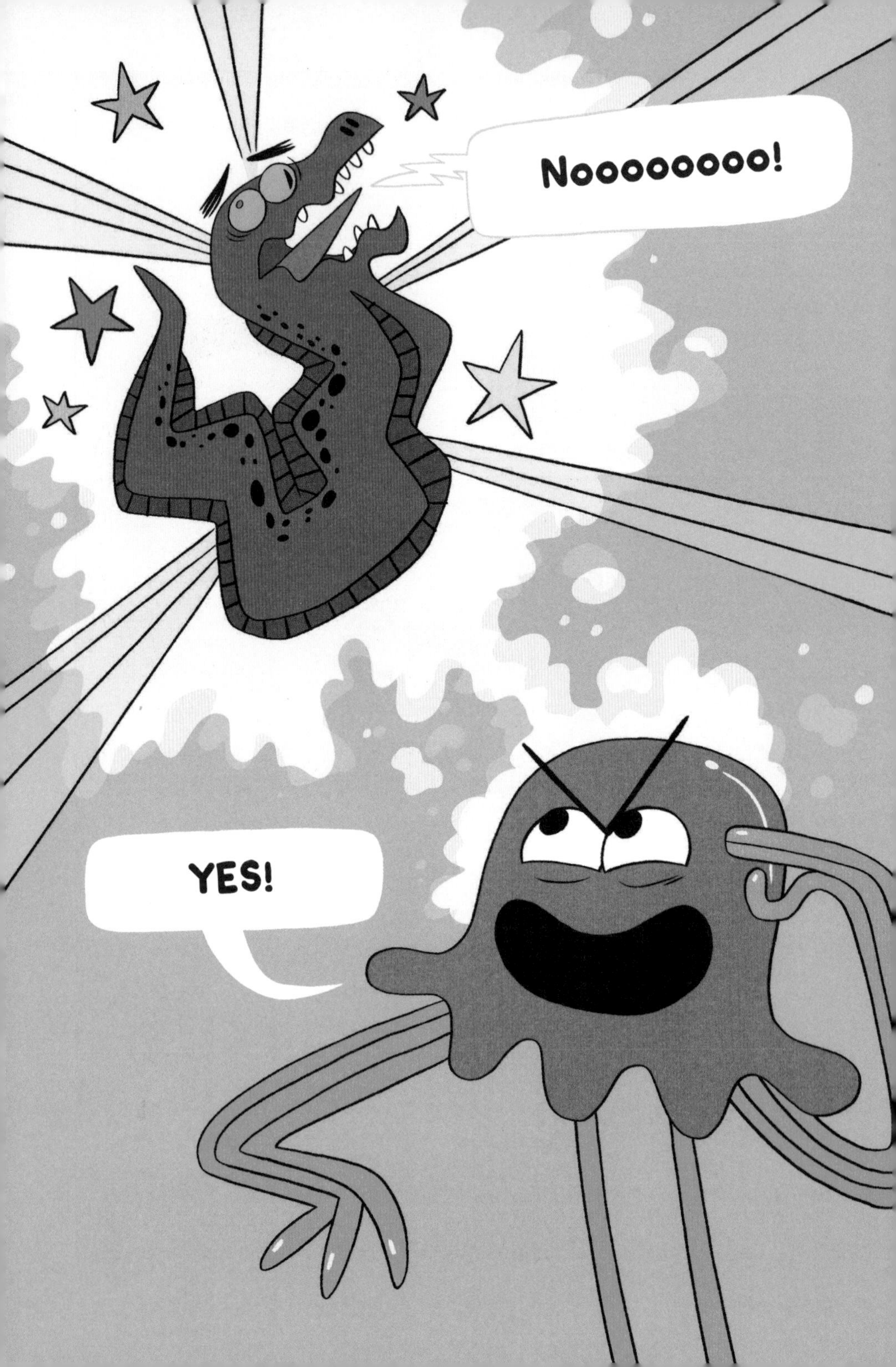
Noooooooo!
YES!

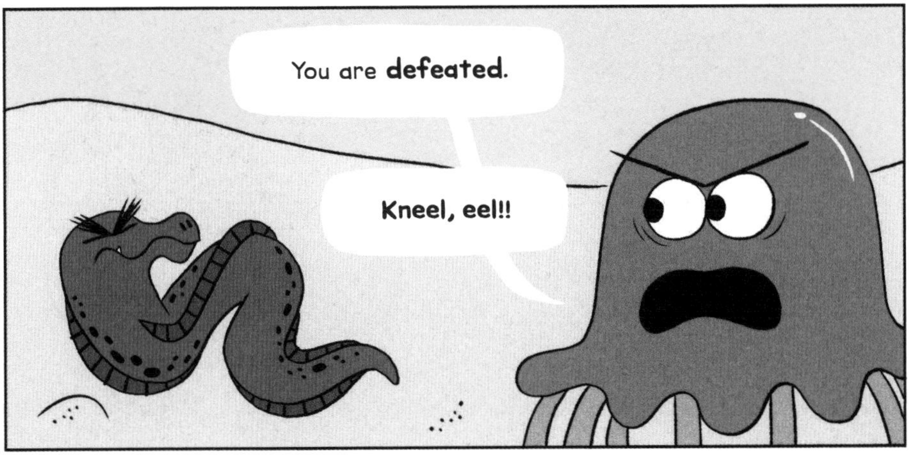
You are **defeated**.
Kneel, eel!!

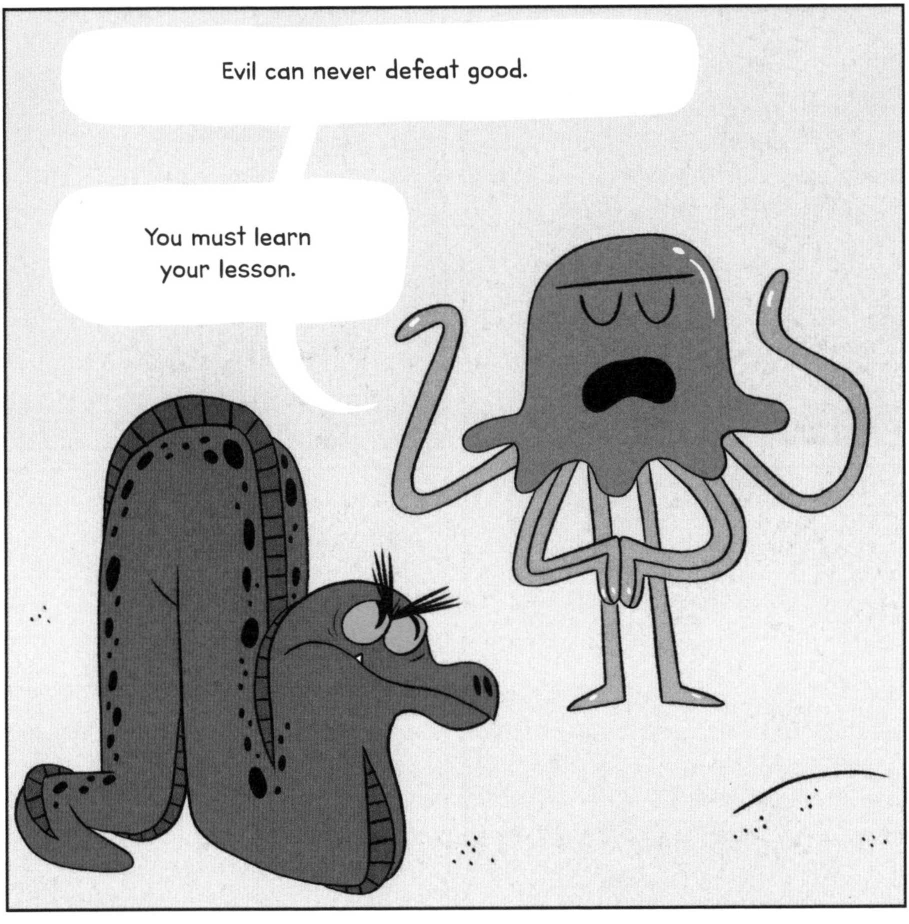
Evil can never defeat good.
You must learn your lesson.

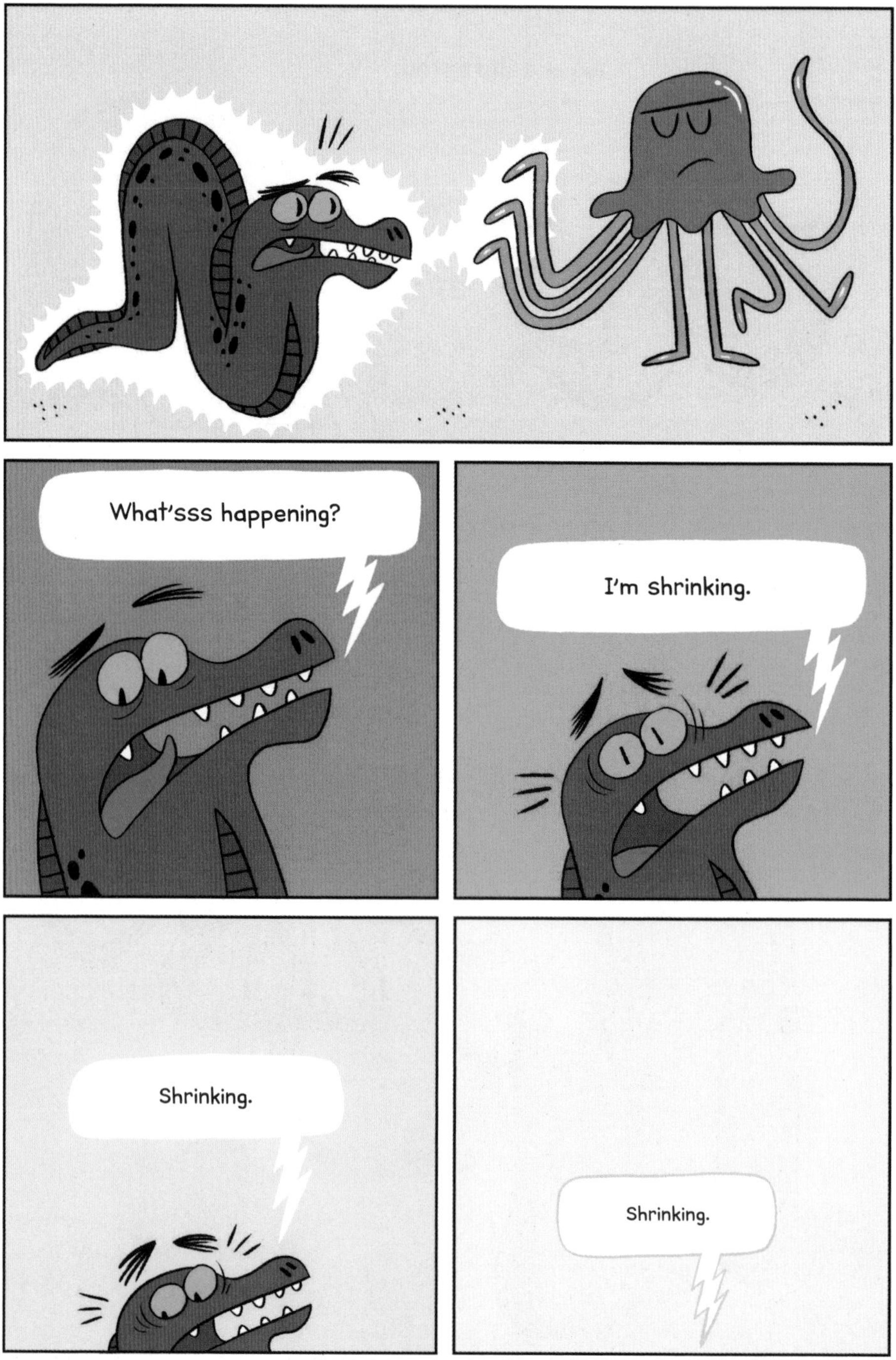
What'sss happening?
I'm shrinking.
Shrinking.
Shrinking.

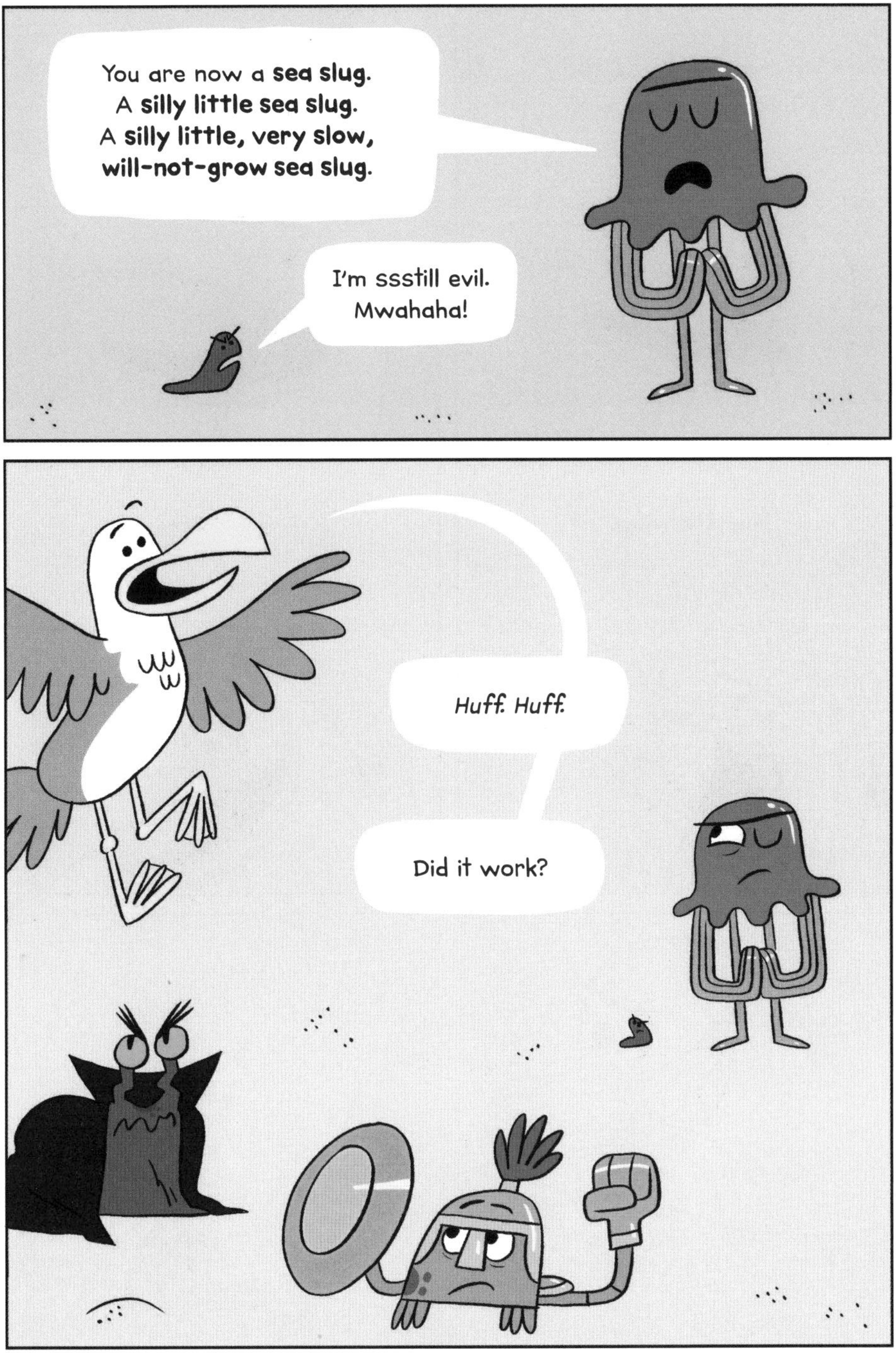
You are now a **sea slug.** A **silly little sea slug.** A **silly little, very slow, will-not-grow sea slug.**
I'm ssstill evil. Mwahaha!
Huff. Huff.
Did it work?

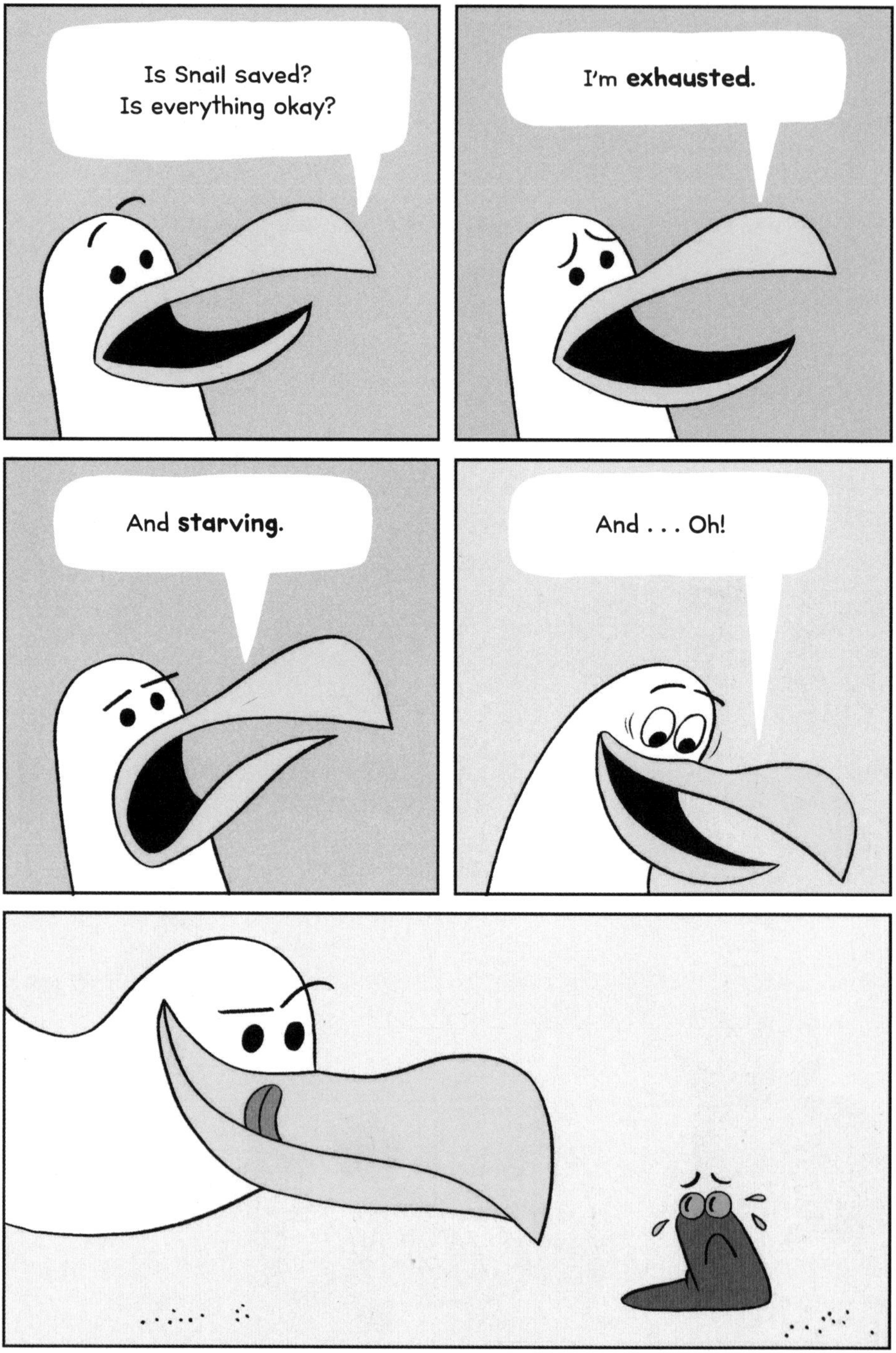
Is Snail saved?
Is everything okay?
I'm **exhausted**.
And **starving**.
And . . . Oh!

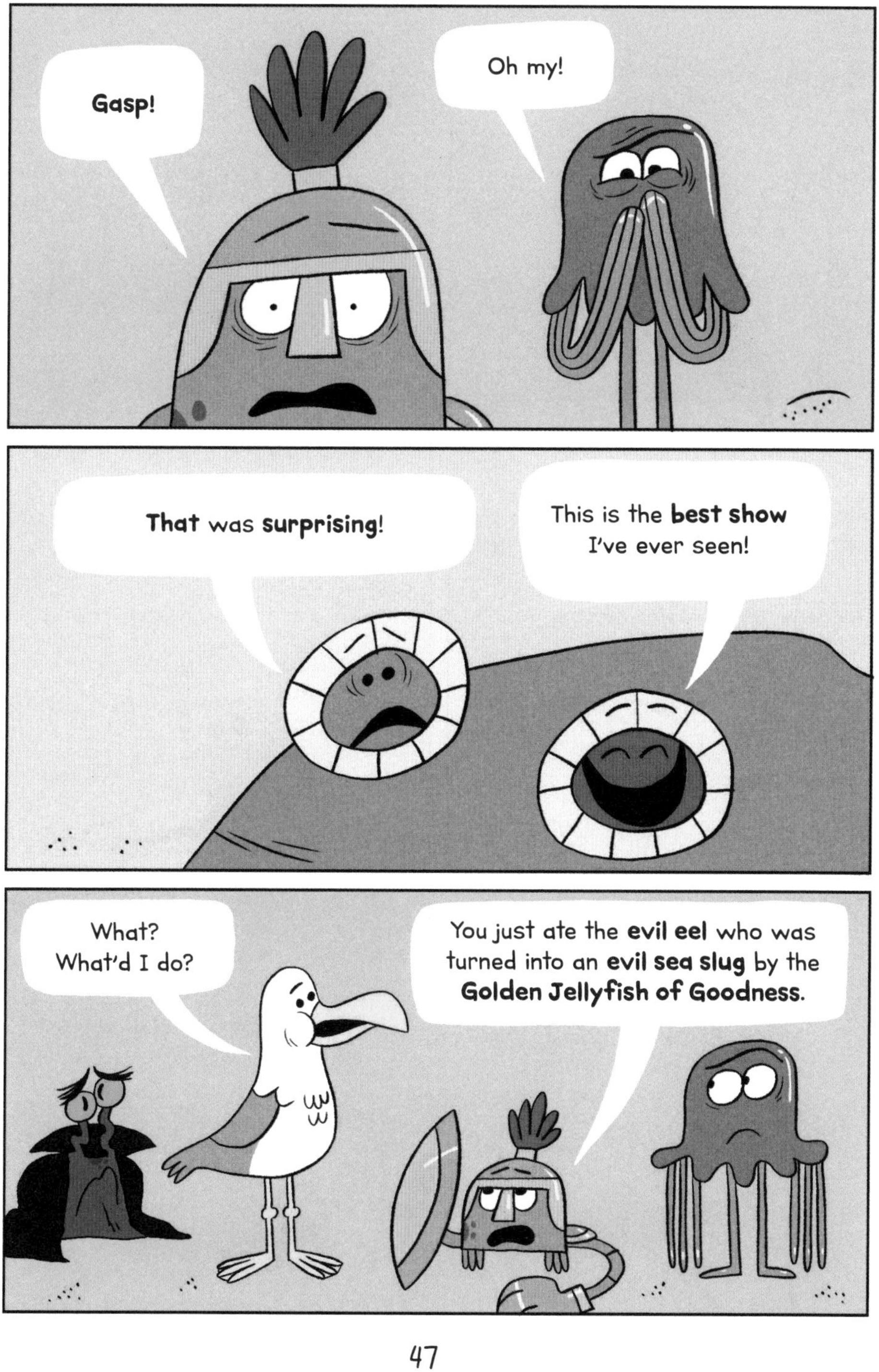
Gasp!
Oh my!
That was surprising!
This is the best show I've ever seen!
What? What'd I do?
You just ate the evil eel who was turned into an evil sea slug by the Golden Jellyfish of Goodness.

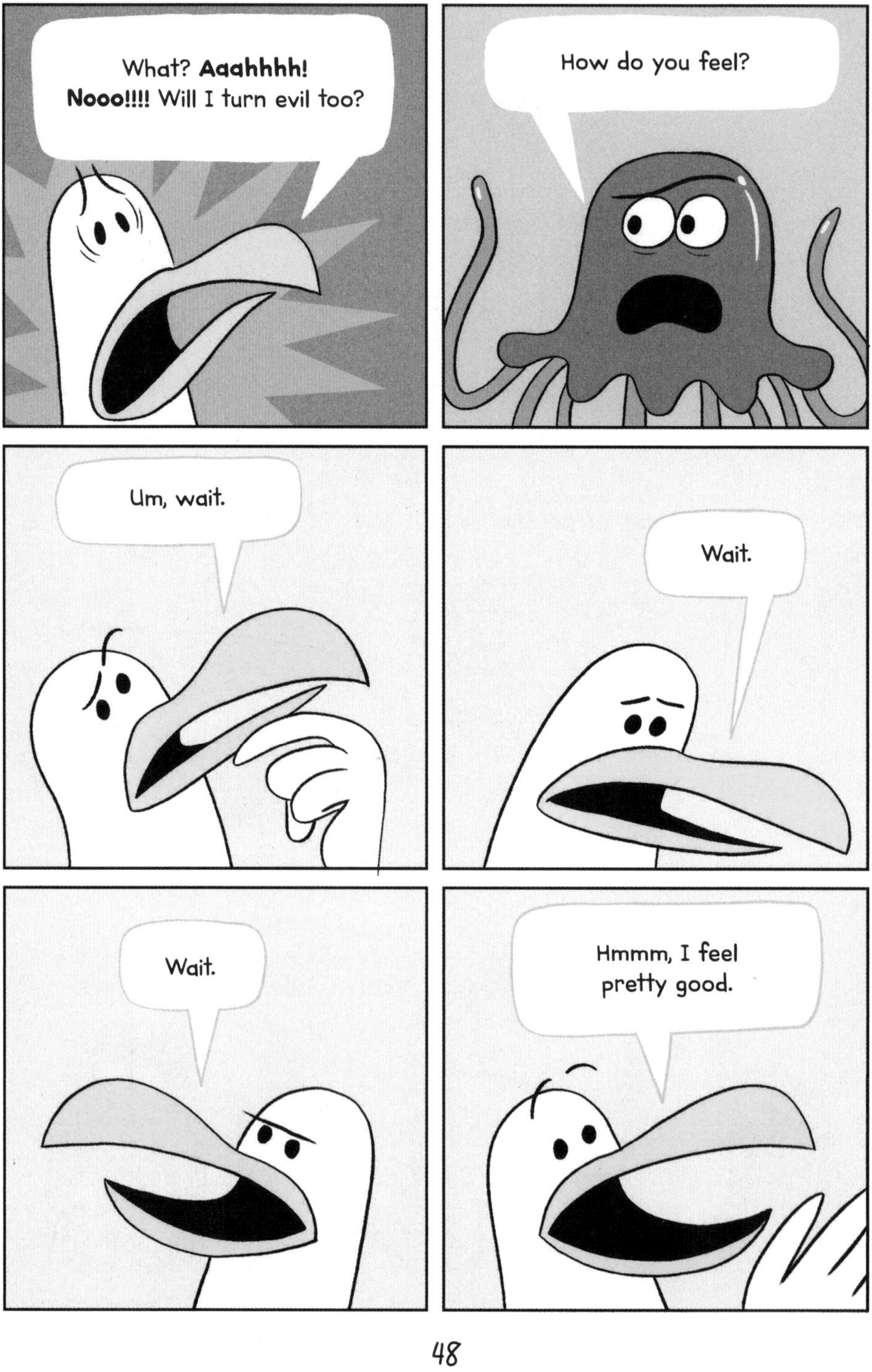
What? **Aaahhhh!** **Nooo!!!!** Will I turn evil too?
How do you feel?
Um, wait.
Wait.
Wait.
Hmmm, I feel pretty good.

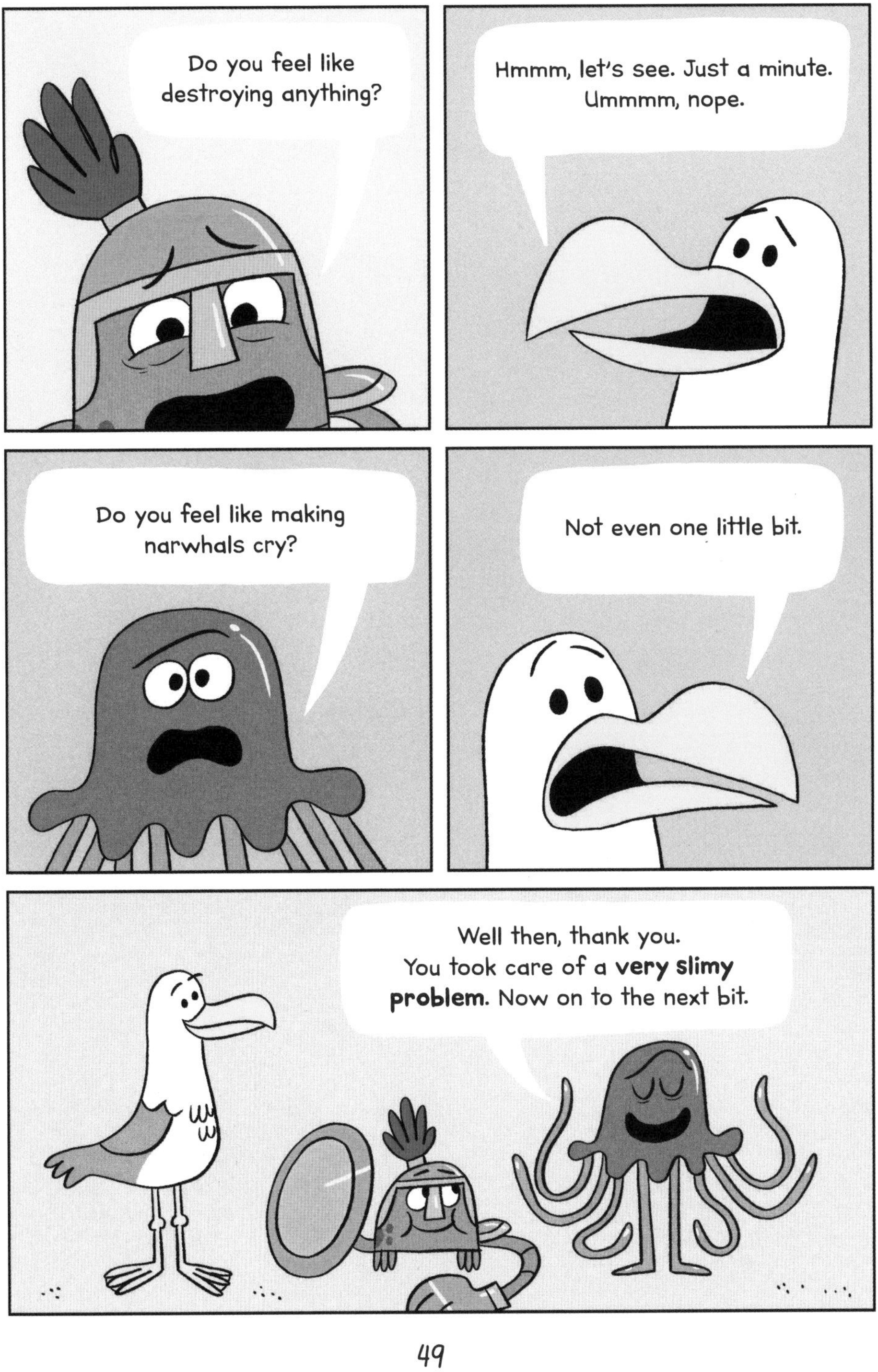
Do you feel like destroying anything?
Hmmm, let's see. Just a minute. Ummmm, nope.
Do you feel like making narwhals cry?
Not even one little bit.
Well then, thank you. You took care of a **very slimy problem**. Now on to the next bit.

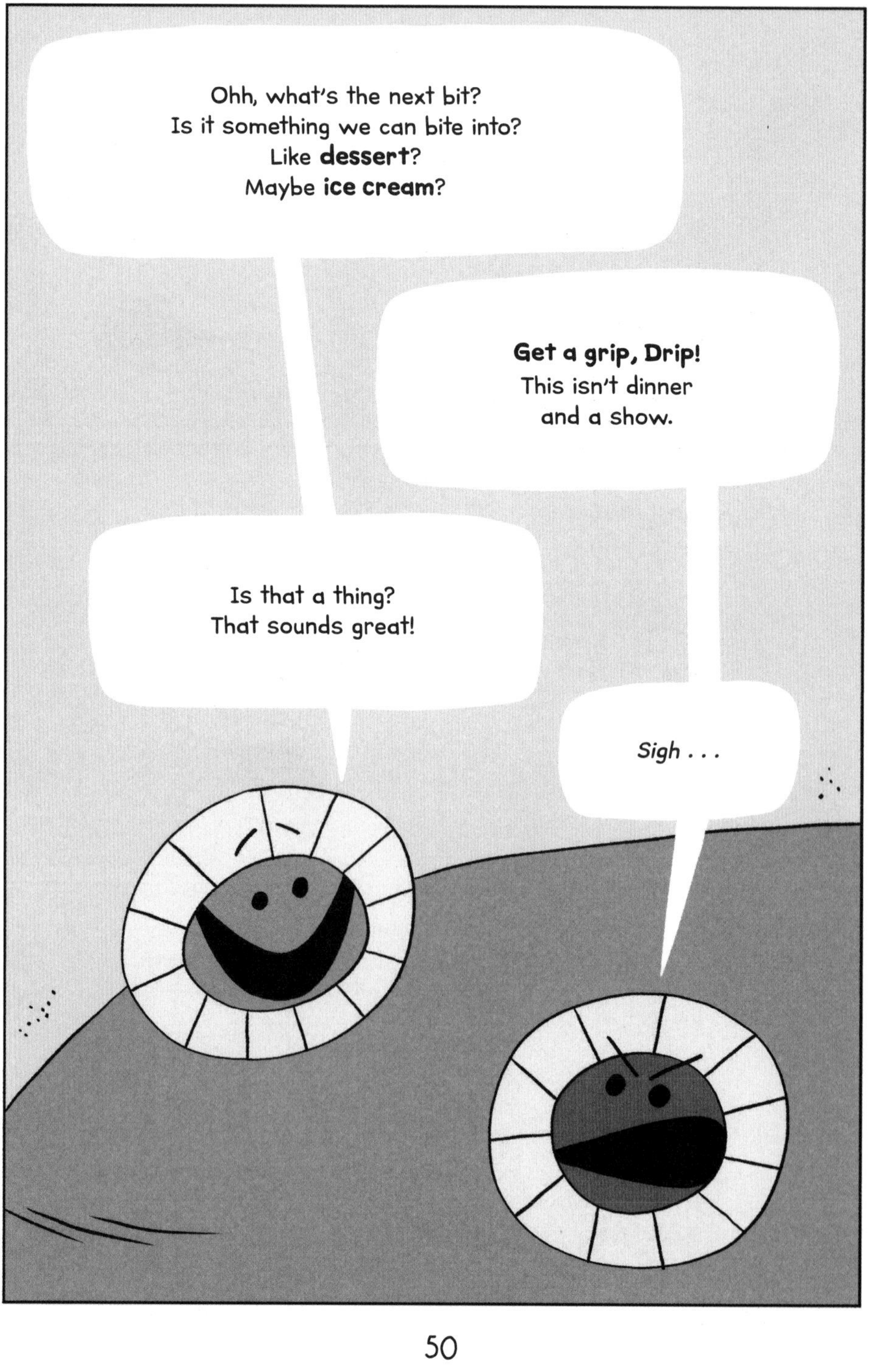
Ohh, what's the next bit? Is it something we can bite into? Like **dessert**? Maybe **ice cream**?
Get a grip, Drip! This isn't dinner and a show.
Is that a thing? That sounds great!
Sigh . . .

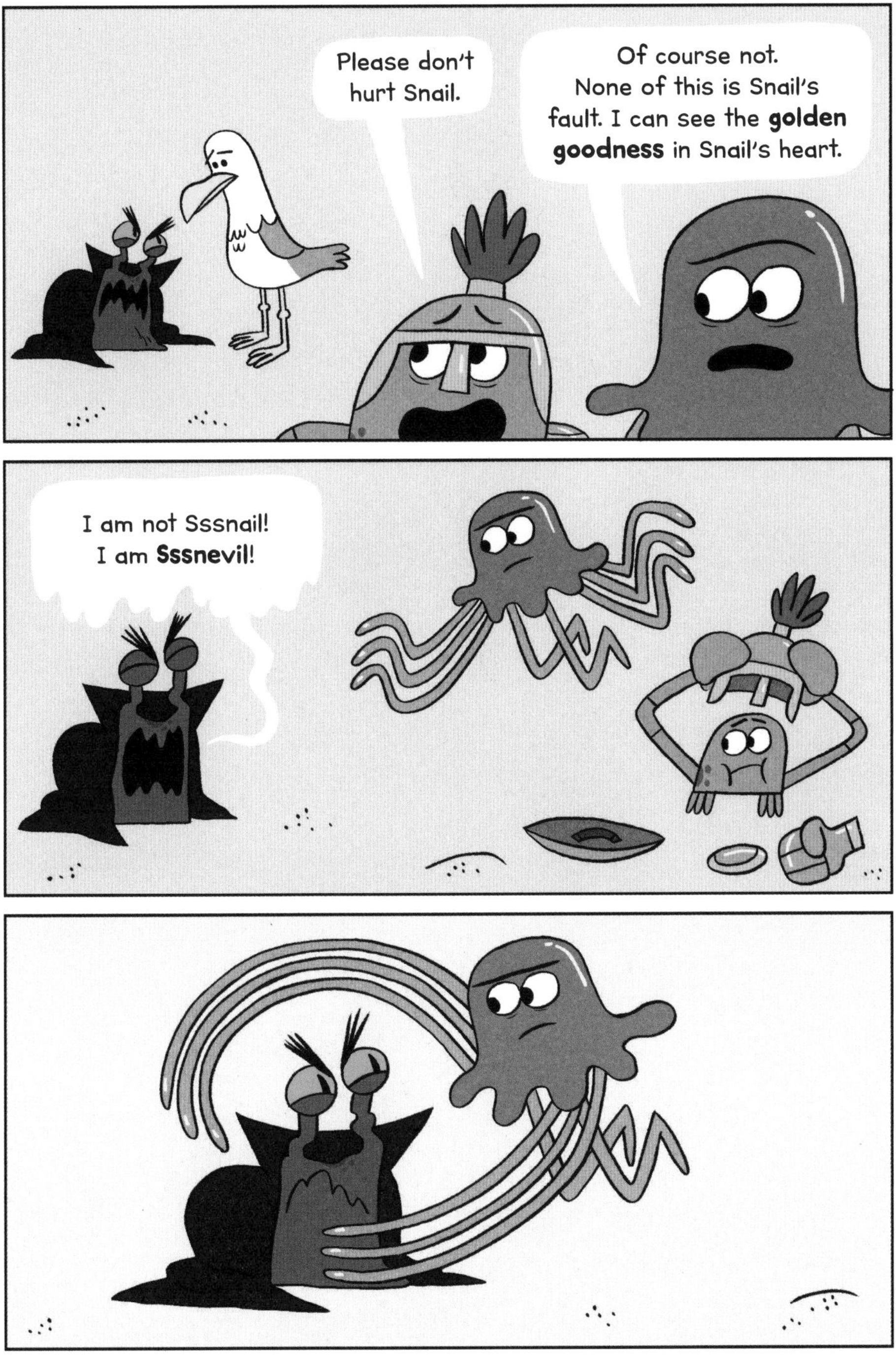
Please don't hurt Snail.
Of course not. None of this is Snail's fault. I can see the **golden goodness** in Snail's heart.
I am not Sssnail! I am **Sssnevil**!

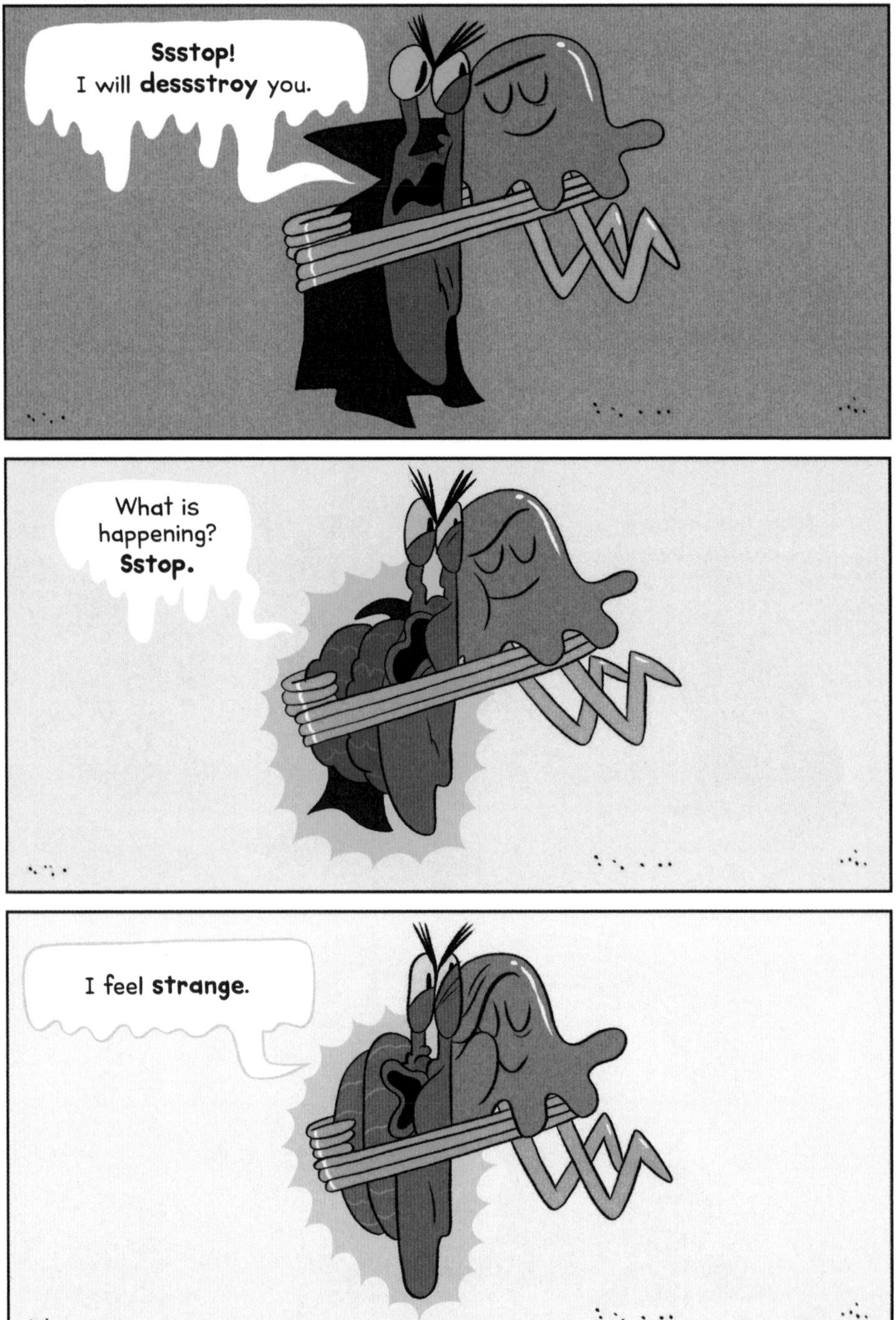
Ssstop!
I will dessstroy you.
What is happening? Sstop.
I feel strange.

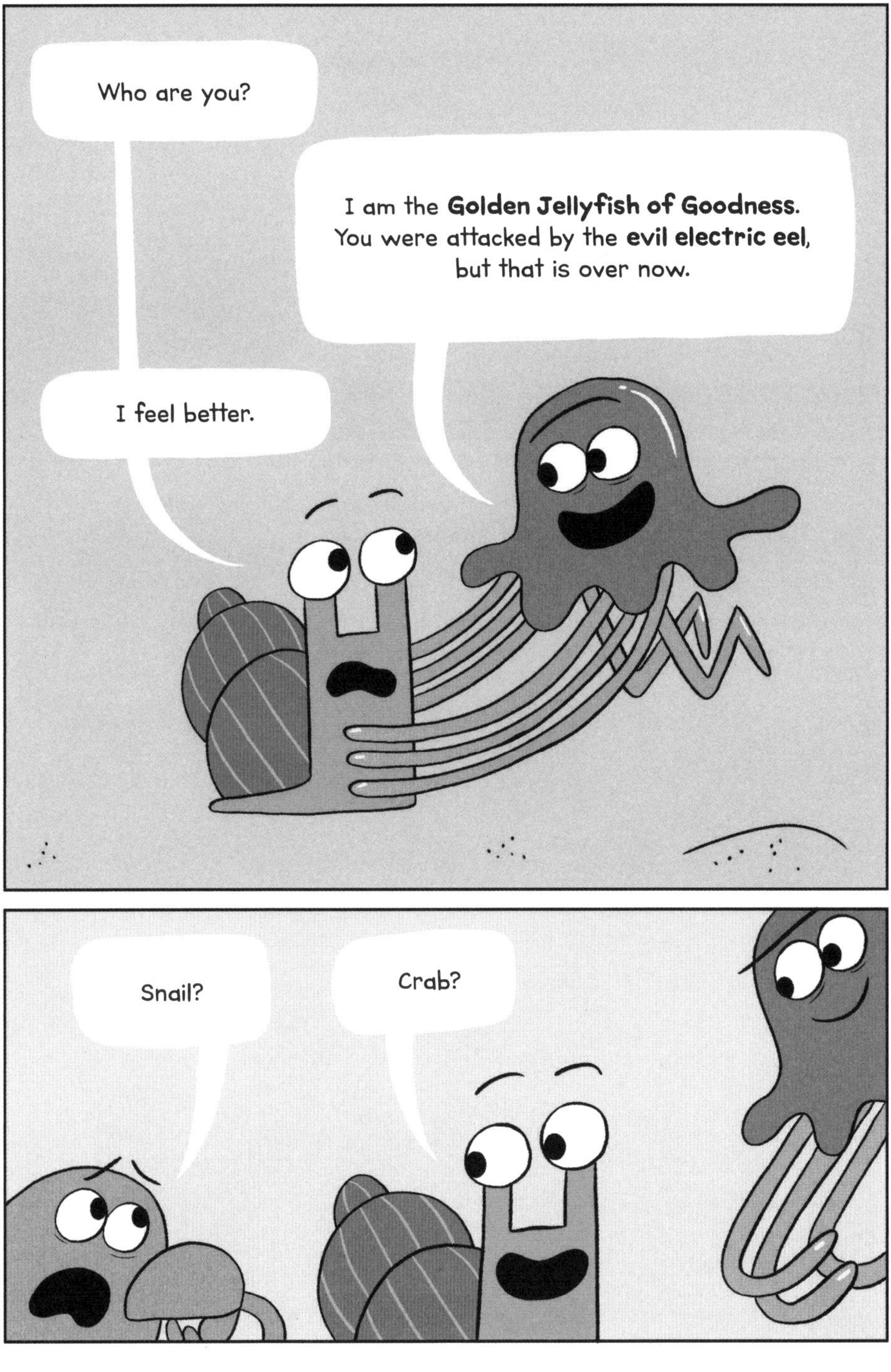
Who are you?
I am the **Golden Jellyfish of Goodness**. You were attacked by the **evil electric eel**, but that is over now.
I feel better.
Snail?
Crab?

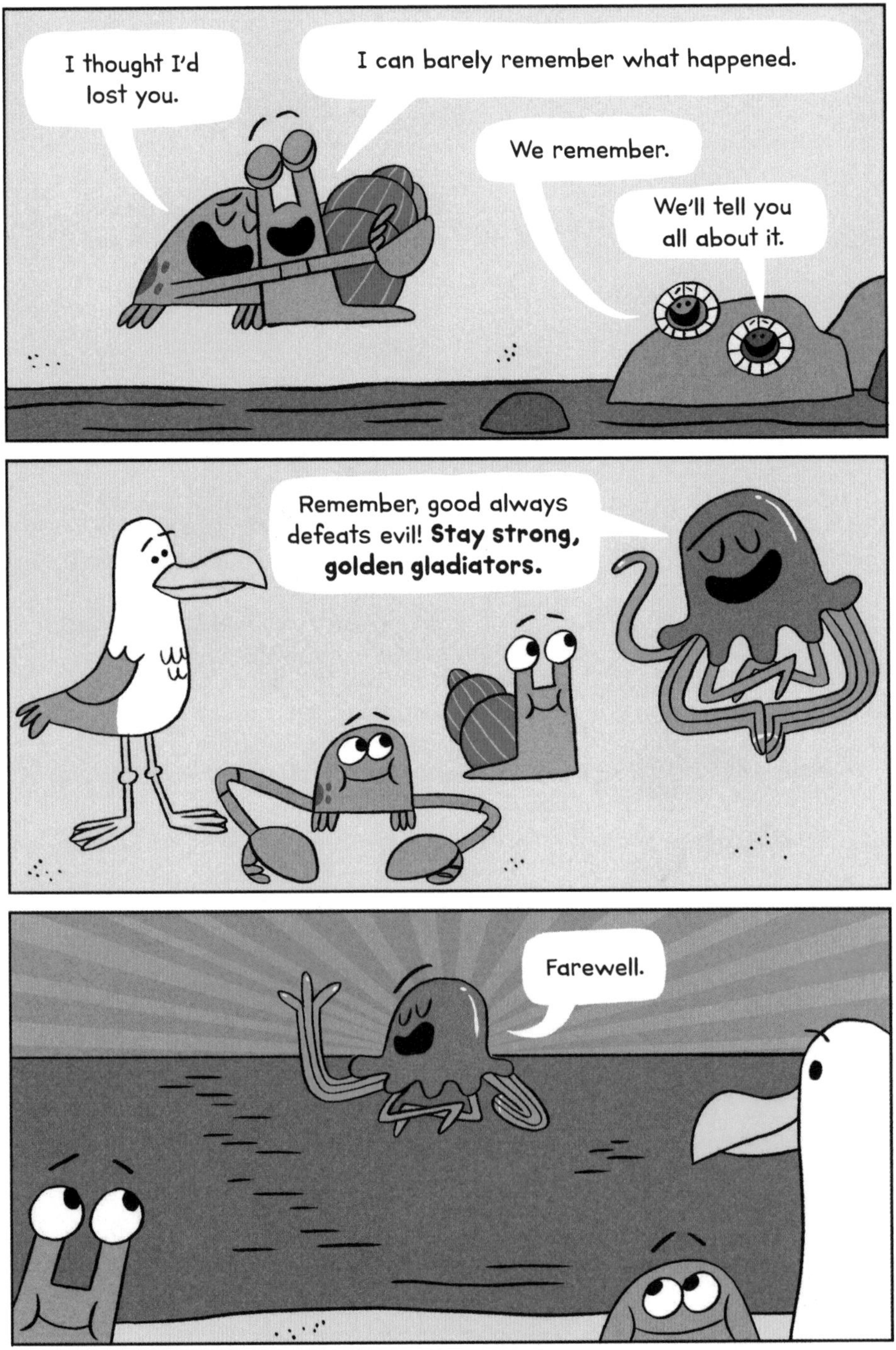
I thought I'd lost you.
I can barely remember what happened.
We remember.
We'll tell you all about it.
Remember, good always defeats evil! **Stay strong, golden gladiators.**
Farewell.

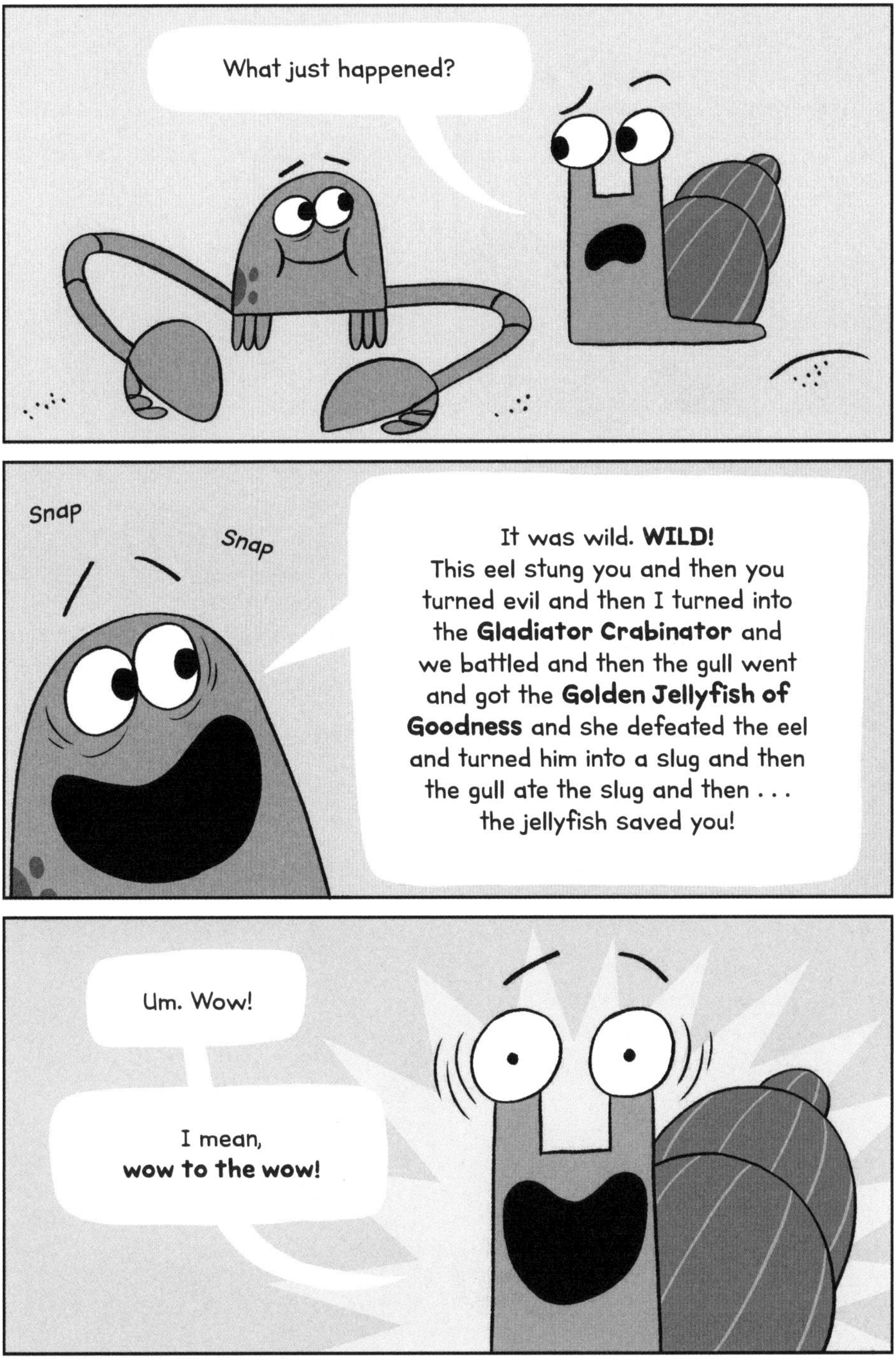
What just happened?
Snap
Snap
It was wild. WILD! This eel stung you and then you turned evil and then I turned into the Gladiator Crabinator and we battled and then the gull went and got the Golden Jellyfish of Goodness and she defeated the eel and turned him into a slug and then the gull ate the slug and then . . . the jellyfish saved you!
Um. Wow!
I mean, wow to the wow!

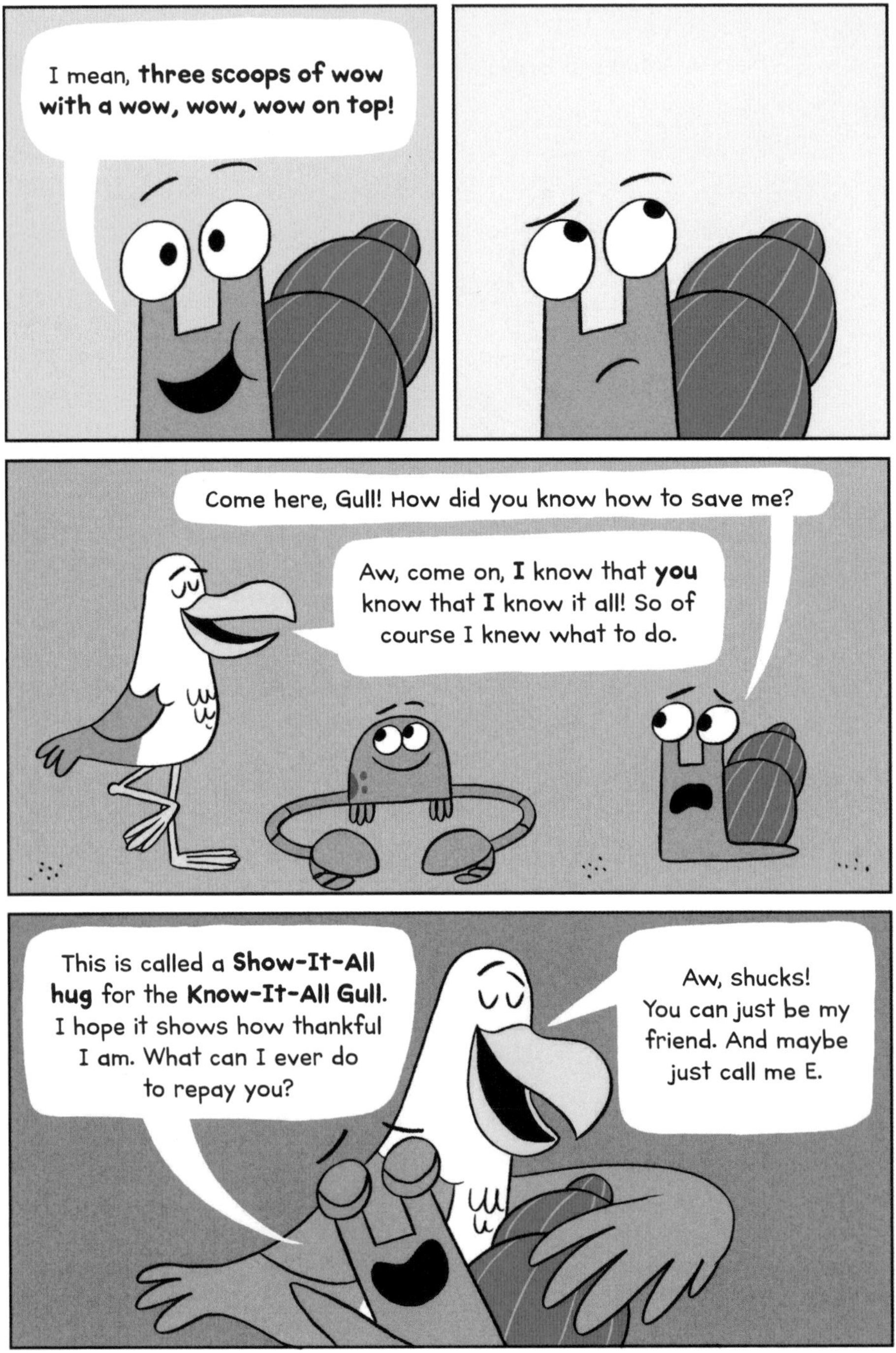

I mean, three scoops of wow with a wow, wow, wow on top!
Come here, Gull! How did you know how to save me?
Aw, come on, I know that you know that I know it all! So of course I knew what to do.
This is called a Show-It-All hug for the Know-It-All Gull. I hope it shows how thankful I am. What can I ever do to repay you?
Aw, shucks! You can just be my friend. And maybe just call me E.

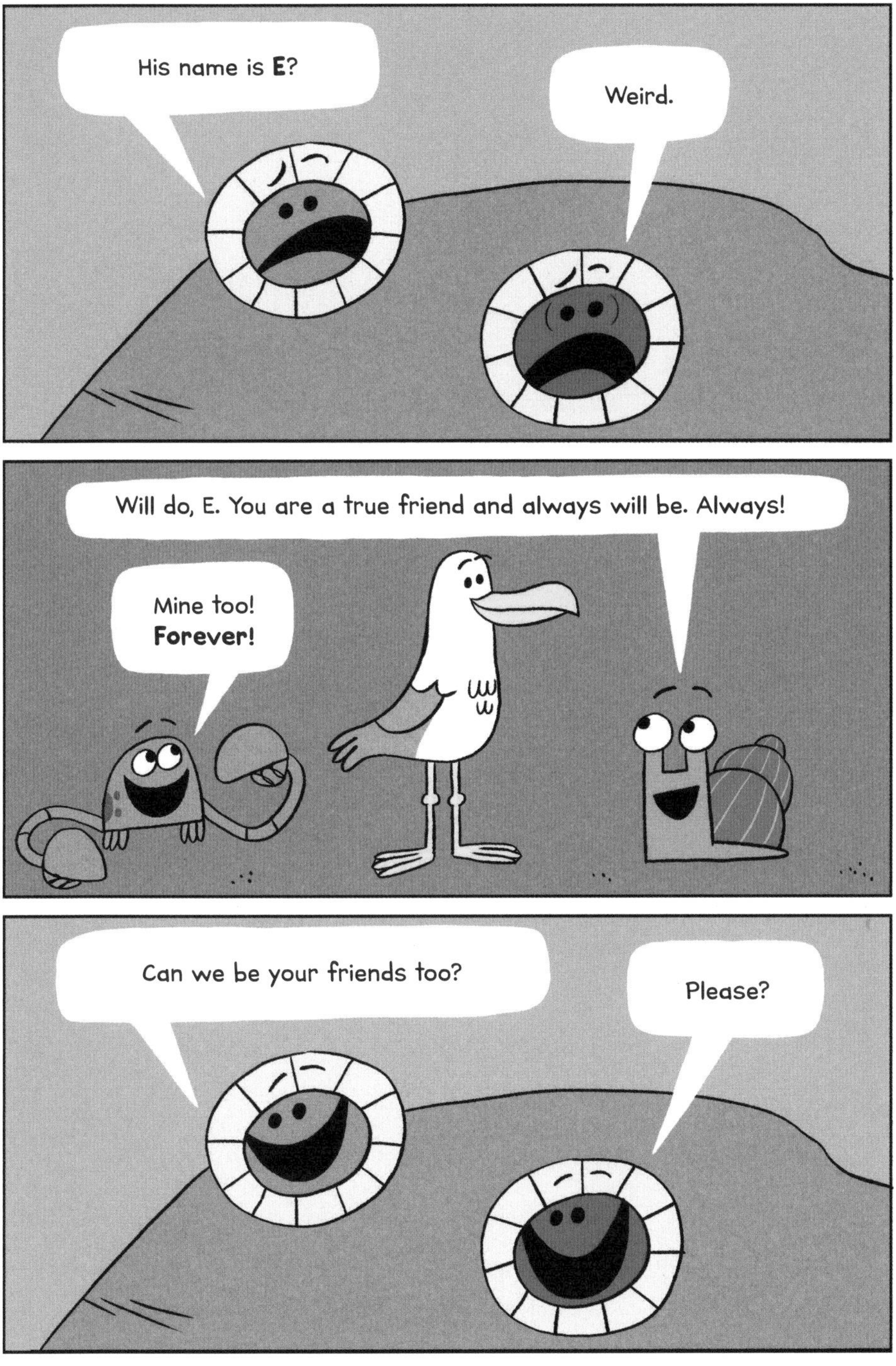
His name is **E**?
Weird.
Will do, E. You are a true friend and always will be. Always!
Mine too! **Forever!**
Can we be your friends too?
Please?

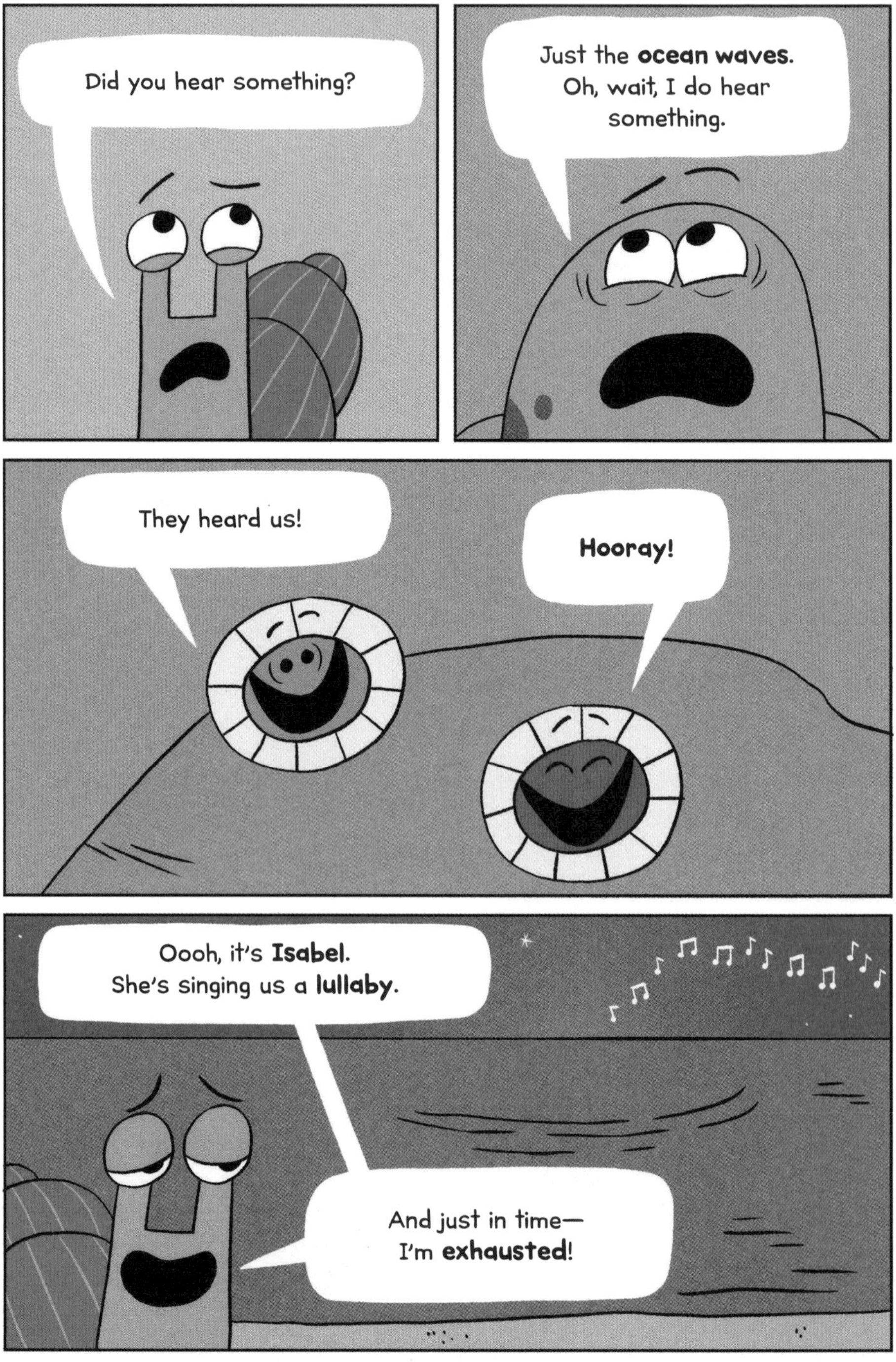
Did you hear something?
Just the **ocean waves.** Oh, wait, I do hear something.
They heard us!
Hooray!
Oooh, it's **Isabel.** She's singing us a **lullaby.**
And just in time— I'm **exhausted!**

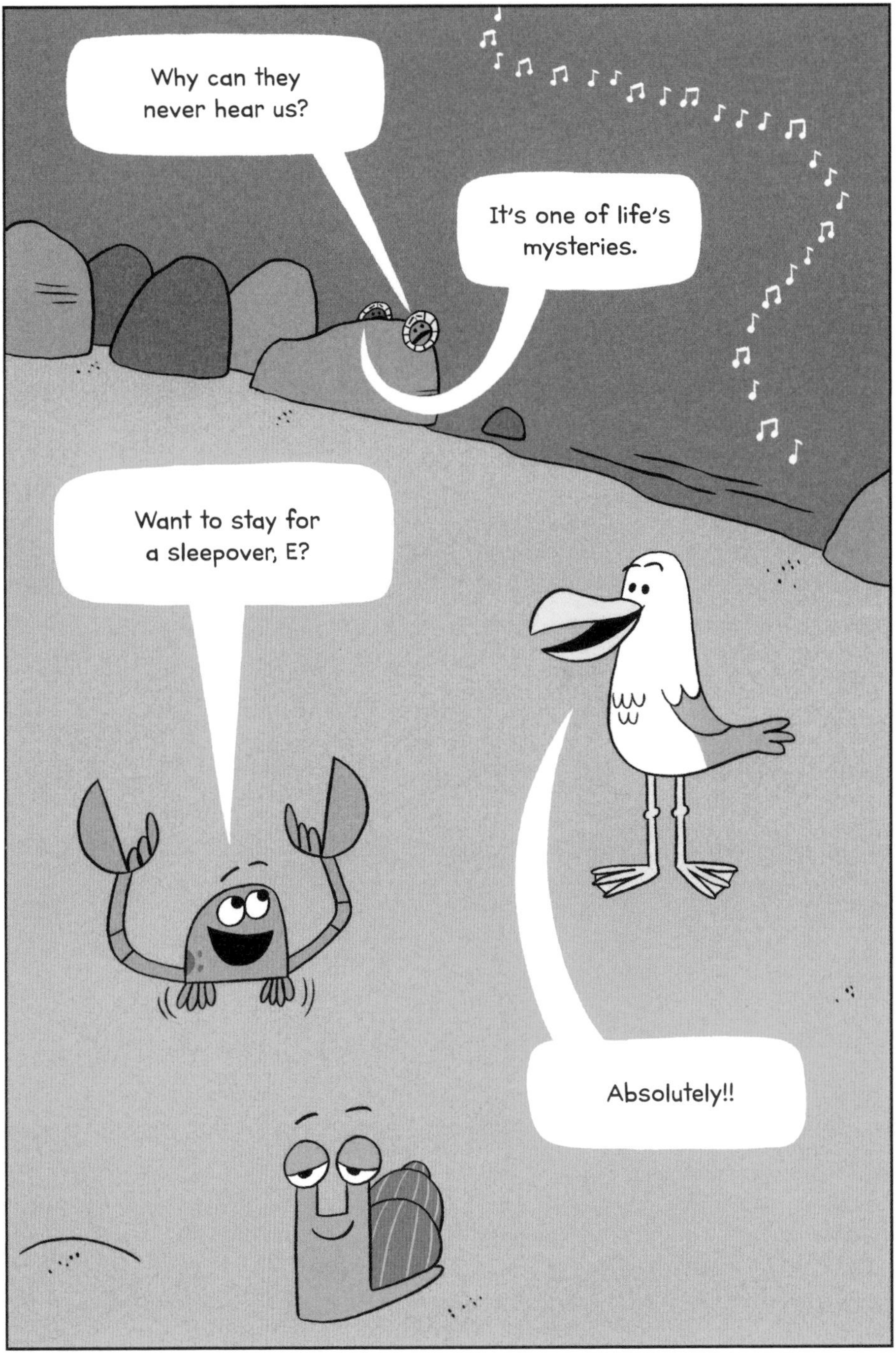
Why can they never hear us?
It's one of life's mysteries.
Want to stay for a sleepover, E?
Absolutely!!

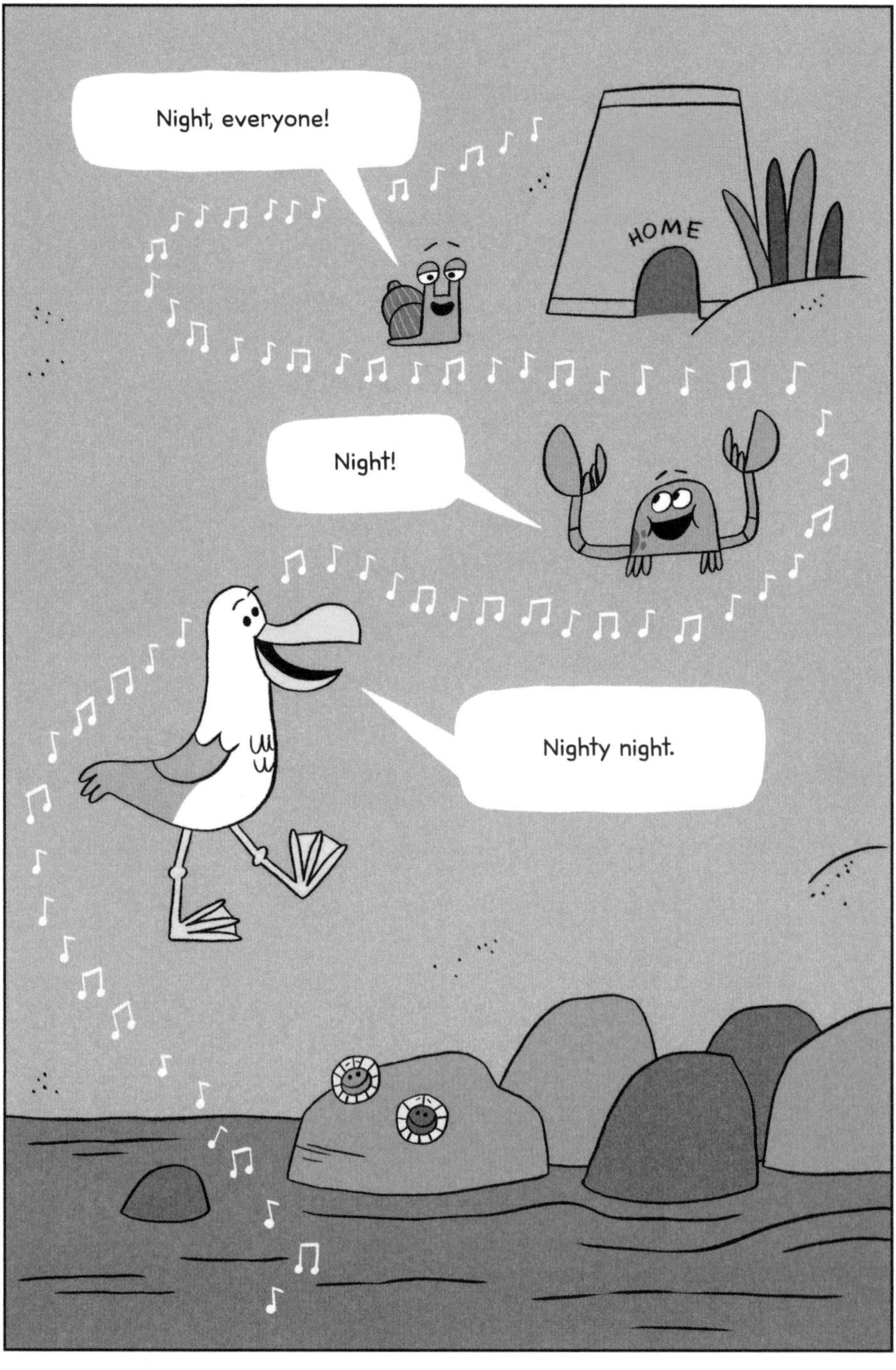
Night, everyone!
HOME
Night!
Nighty night.

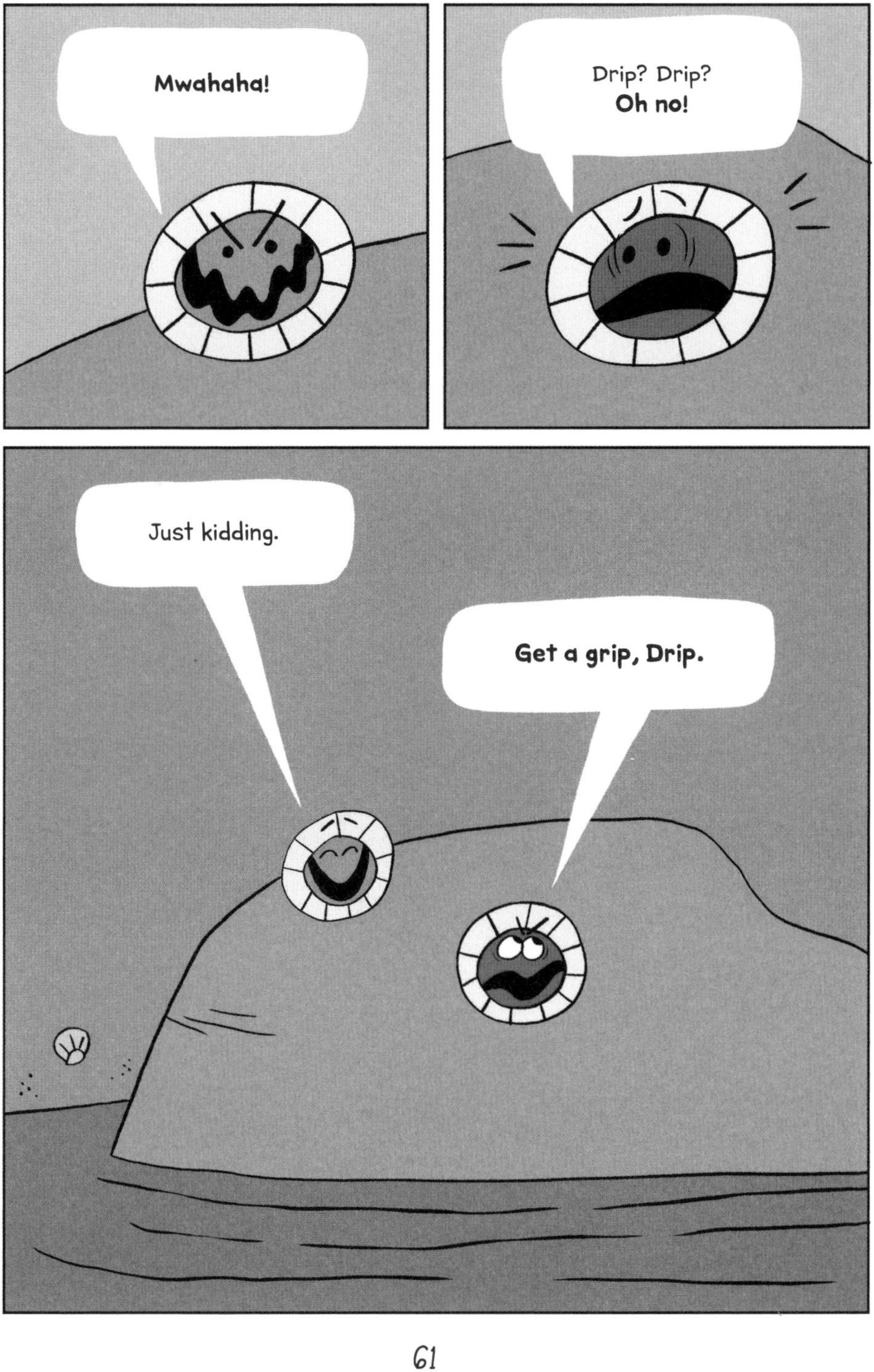
Mwahaha!
Drip? Drip? Oh no!
Just kidding.
Get a grip, Drip.

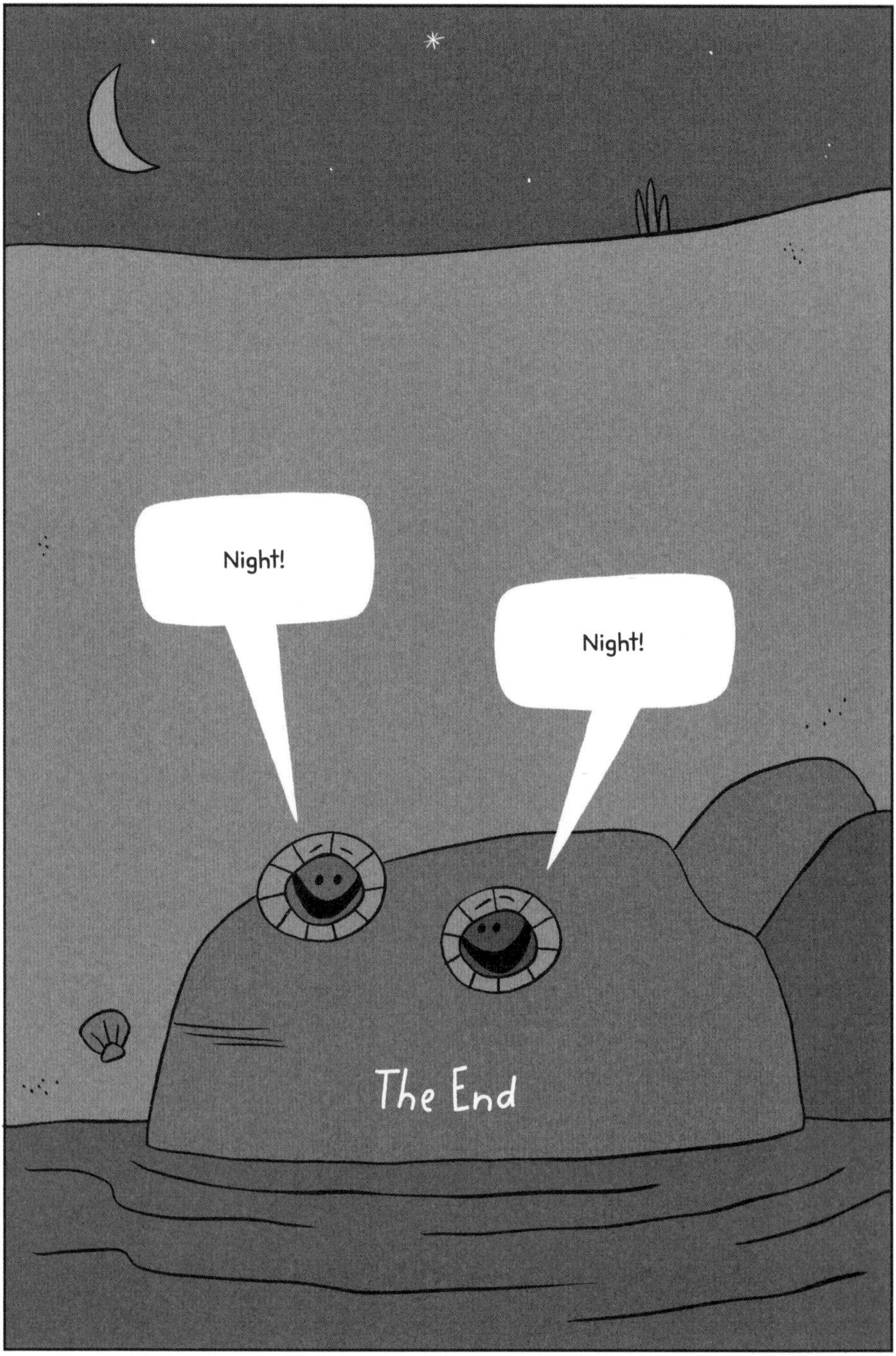
Night!
Night!
The End

Don't miss Crab and Snail's
other seaside adventures!

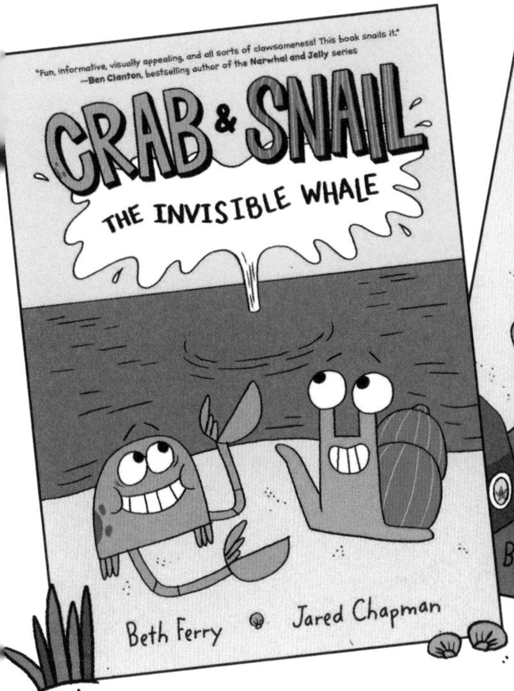
"Fun, informative, visually appealing, and all sorts of clawsomeness! This book snails it."
—Ben Clanton, bestselling author of the Narwhal and Jelly series
CRAB & SNAIL
THE INVISIBLE WHALE
Beth Ferry
Jared Chapman

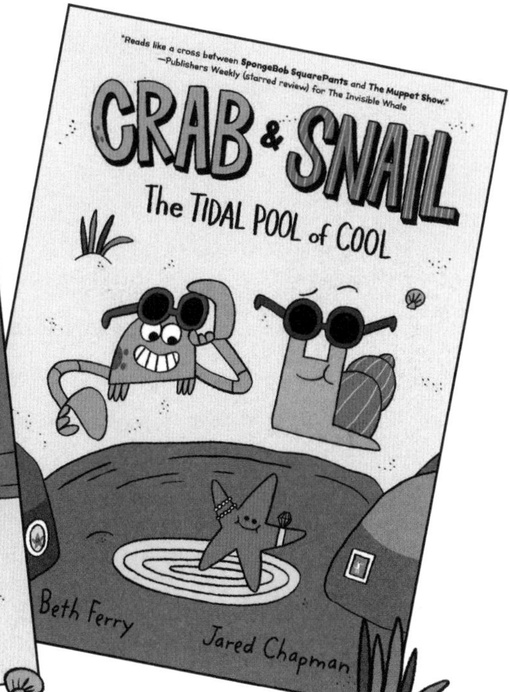
"Reads like a cross between SpongeBob SquarePants and The Muppet Show."
—Publishers Weekly (starred review) for The Invisible Whale
CRAB & SNAIL
The TIDAL POOL of COOL
Beth Ferry
Jared Chapman

Beth Ferry lives by the beach in New Jersey where she has shared her home with a myriad of aquatic creatures, including a lionfish, a clownfish, a pufferfish, several seahorses, and one beautiful snowflake eel. Luckily for her, the eel wasn't evil. Not even a little. He was, in fact, quite shy and quiet, making him the perfect fish tank pet. Beth enjoys writing about pets and friendship and anything that has to do with the ocean. You can learn more at bethferry.com.

Jared Chapman is the author and illustrator of books such as *Vegetables in Underwear*; *T. Rex Time Machine*; and *Steve, Raised By Wolves*. Jared lives with his wife and four kids in Northeast Texas, which is very far from the ocean, so when his kids say things like, "Dad is mean! He was probably tagged by an evil eel!," don't believe them. Visit him online at jaredchapman.com.